The Streets Keep Calling

The Streets Keep Calling

Chunichi

URBAN BOOKS

www.urbanbooks.net

Urban Books, LLC
97 N18th Street
Wyandanch, NY 11798

The Streets Keep Calling © Copyright 2010 Chunichi

ISBN 13: 978-1-60162-570-0
ISBN 10: 1-60162-570-7

First Mass Market Paperback Printing November 2013
First Trade Paperback Printing December 2010
Printed in the United States of America

10 9 8 7 6 5 4 3

*This is a work of fiction. Any references or similarities
to actual events, real people, living or dead, or to real
locales are intended to give the novel a sense of reality.
Any similarity in other names, characters, places, and
incidents is entirely coincidental.*

Distributed by Kensington Publishing Corp.
Submit Wholesale Orders to:
Kensington Publishing Corp.
C/O Penguin Group (USA) Inc.
Attention: Order Processing
405 Murray Hill Parkway
East Rutherford, NJ 07073-2316
Phone: 1-800-526-0275
Fax: 1-800-227-9604

Chapter 1

Free at Last
Breeze

"Free at last. Free at last. Thank God Almighty, I'm free at last," I shouted at the top of my lungs. I walked out the gates of the federal penitentiary after serving five long years for drug charges.

From the first day I'd begun serving my time I'd been waiting for the day I would be released. I walked out the gates with the same thug stroll I'd had walking into the courtroom, and, ultimately, into the brick walls of the federal penitentiary. I walked proud with my head high and a mean grit. No one would have ever known that I ain't have shit, not even a hundred dollars to my name. A nigga would think I had the same half a million dollars cash and even more in assets that I'd originally had when I first got locked up. One thing about me though, I am always one of two things: either filthy rich or dead broke.

"Goddamn!" I said, realizing there was no one outside waiting to pick me up.

I scanned the parking lot again, looking to my left, then looking to my right. Still I ain't see no one. Other than a couple of cars parked in the visitor parking area, there wasn't a single nigga there but me. Even though I knew not to expect any of my boys to be there waiting to pick me up, it still hurt like a bitch to come out to nothing. At that point I ain't have no one. The so-called boys who didn't snitch on me or steal from me forgot about me after the third year of my bid. We all know how the saying goes: "out of sight, out of mind." In my case, it's been proven.

Before I got locked up, I had a whole crew of niggas by my side and another list of niggas who wished they could be by my side. But when shit got hot, niggas started snitching to save their own asses. The niggas who ain't have shit until I took them under my wing were the same bitch-ass niggas who turned on me. As soon as they felt a little bit of pressure, they were quick to drop names and information. Then there were those who owed me money before I got locked up. These niggas saw that as a free ticket. I had cats making promises to pay my lawyer, give money to my moms, and look out for my wife and kids with the money they owed. Needless to say, my lawyer, mother, and wife and kids never saw a single dollar of that money.

As far as my wife, Maria, and kids, Jaden and Kaylyn, go, well, deep inside I knew they wouldn't be waiting outside the gates for me either. Even though I hoped and prayed I would walk out those gates and be greeted by them running into my arms, I knew I was wishing on a star. Maria had turned her back on me a long time ago. Despite that I had left everything I owned to her.

At the time I got locked up, we were the picture-perfect happy family living in a $300,000 house that was paid for. My wife had her own personal car, we had a family truck, and I had over $500,000 stashed up in cash. When I went in to do my time, I made sure everything was taken care of for her. I had my attorney sign over all my paperwork so she could have access to and be in control of all my assets, and I gave her all my drug money down to the last dollar. It never crossed my mind that she would be the type of woman to turn her back on me, her husband, of all people. I figured with the house, cars, and money, she'd be straight and wait for me until I got out. Even that wasn't enough to keep her.

I will never forget the pain I felt when I called my house number collect, and the operator told me the charges were denied. I must have tried calling at least two times a day for, like, two weeks straight just to make sure I had the right number. I couldn't understand for the life of me why my wife would not take my call. Then one day I called and the operator said that the number was disconnected. When I heard that ma'fucking disconnected recording come on, I was pissed. Then I felt betrayed, but beyond all that, I was hurt that my wife would do something like that to me. After all the shit I had done to make sure she and the kids were taken care of, she would turn her back on me like that? But then I convinced myself that she had a perfectly good explanation for changing the number. It dawned on me that she might have gotten wind that the line was tapped, and she didn't want to talk to me on it. I figured instead of getting pissed off, I would just wait for a letter from her with the new number and an explanation; but that letter never came. It didn't even take her one year to change her number, stop visiting, and stop sending letters.

I can't lie; I didn't have an easy bid. I knew things weren't gonna be easy from the first day I walked through the prison gates. On the streets I had a crew, a gun, and a whole lot of hood respect. I'd spent years proving I was gangster, but once I was behind those prison walls, I was a nobody with an assigned number. After all the sacrifice and time it took me to get to the top of the street game, I walked into that place and had to work my way from the bottom up and gain my respect all over again. I got in countless fights, losing more than I won. Hell, I was stabbed the first week, and put in the hole a few weeks after that. I lost my good time for getting caught with a cell phone, and even had a couple incidents that I've constantly tried to erase from my memory. Even through all that, nothing hurt me as bad as being away from my kids. No lie, not being able to see or talk to my kids was the hardest part of my entire bid.

Realizing there wasn't a person in sight to pick me up, I finally said, "fuck it," and started to walk. I had already made my mind up while I was in prison: I was gonna come out a new person. No more of the bullshit that got me locked up. I wanted one thing and one thing only, and that was to get my wife and kids back. I didn't give a fuck what it would take, I was gonna get them back and never leave them again. I had plans to work a nine-to-five, see my parole officer as instructed, get my rights back, get some credit, and live the simple life.

I hadn't taken a good three steps when a familiar car rolled up. I couldn't do anything but shake my head and smile, as Moms pulled up in my 2002 Lexus GS 300.

"What the fuck?" I had to laugh. This shit I was looking at was crazy!

As Moms rolled up, all I could see was her blond wig, long acrylic nails, and cigarette smoke escaping from the driver's side window. I looked at my car as she got closer. There was a dent in the side, a number of scratches and dings, and, worst of all, Moms was rolling on three custom rims and one factory rim: straight hood!

"There's my baby boy." Moms flicked her cigarette butt out the window and hopped out of the car. She ran and jumped her teeny five feet two petite frame into my arms. I stood over six feet tall, towering over her. I lifted her off her feet, hugging her tight. "I missed you so much," she said with tears of joy in her eyes as she kissed me on the cheek. It took me back years. I felt like I was five years old again.

"Come on, Ma. Ain't no need for crying. I'm home now." I dried the tears from my mom's face and we headed to the car. When I got in the passenger's side, I couldn't believe the inside of the car was worse than the outstide. My leather was scratched and ripped, the steering wheel stitching was holding on for dear life, and my GPS screen was cracked.

"Ma, what happened to my car? It looks like Hurricane Katrina ripped through it! You couldn't take better care of it?" I knew Ma was never one to care much about cars but poor "Lexy," as I used to call her, looked so bad, not even a crackhead would consider breaking into her.

"Breeze, I know I didn't just take an unpaid day off of work to come and pick your behind up for you to question me about no damn car, boy! You can walk home if you don't like what you see!" she said, smirking, knowing I didn't have much of a choice but to shut up and take it.

"Whatever, Ma! Take me to see my kids," I commanded.

"Lord, Breeze, I don't know why you don't just leave that girl alone. She took all your money and turned her back on you while you were in jail. Now she out there running around with some old rich man they call Mr. Biggs. That girl has always been about money. Boy, you ain't realized that yet?" my mom said, full of attitude.

Moms ain't never liked Maria. She felt Maria always thought she was better than our family. Maria grew up with a silver spoon in her mouth. She went to the best schools, had the best clothes, and rubbed shoulders with people in high places. She had a master's degree in psychology but never worked a day in her life. Her mother was a Spanish woman who worked as a school superintendent. Her father was a white man who owned a construction company that was contracted with the government to build government buildings.

Now you compare that to the life I and my family knew. Moms was a single mother from the day I was born. I ain't never knew my daddy, and I ain't sure if he ever knew about me either. According to my grandmother, my moms was crazy in love with Daddy from the first day they met. They spent every minute they could together until she got pregnant. My grandmother said she never asked what happened between them, but all she knew was that my moms got pregnant and he was gone. My grandmother told me my moms fell into a deep depression after that. She did the best she could to raise me, while Moms spent countless nights drinking and hanging out at the clubs. As much as she tried to keep up with me, I was never home. I grew up in the projects, and was practically raised by the streets. School was never my thing, so I dropped out as soon as I was old enough, and started my hustle on the streets. Before I knew it, I was hood rich. That's right, I had riches, just as much as Maria's family, but I got my riches solely from selling drugs. As Moms said, Maria was about the dollars. If not for those riches, I would have never pulled a girl like Maria, or had her hand in marriage.

"I just wanna see my kids, Ma," I said, even though deep inside I wanted to see Maria just as bad.

"Well, you gonna have to find that girl first. She sold the house."

"She did what?" I couldn't believe what my mom was saying to me.

"You heard me." Ma pulled out a Newport and lit it. "That greedy, money-hungry, mixed-breed bitch sold the damn house, Breeze. She left me and your grandma cramped up in that old house in the hood. That mixed breed sold that big-ass house you left her! Why you so worried about her anyway? You need to be worried about how you gonna live cause we both know that drug shit didn't work out too good for you the last time. While you thinking about that, think about where you gonna live, 'cause we both know Momma's house is too small for all of us," my moms ranted.

"What? When? Why you ain't tell me?" I asked, only caring about the house and totally ignoring my moms, other statements.

"Breeze, did you hear anything I just said to you about how and where you gonna live?"

"Yeah, but that's not important to me right now. Why didn't you tell me Maria sold the house?" I redirected my moms back to the house situation.

"I didn't want you to worry while you were locked up. You had enough things on your mind." Moms took a long pull off her cigarette, then blew the smoke out the window.

I couldn't believe Maria would stoop that low. I bought that house because she wanted it so bad. Everything in there she handpicked: furniture, appliances, carpet, all the way down to the fucking light fixtures. Then as soon as a nigga got locked up, she sold the shit! The more I thought about that shit, the angrier I got. I spent the rest of the ride deep in thought.

"We're home," my mom said, breaking me out of my trance.

I shook my head as we pulled up to my grand-mother's house. I was back to the same place I'd started from. The same damn ghetto I grew up in, and the same old-ass house with broken shutters and chipped paint. It was like I was sixteen years old all over again. I glanced around my hood, and all that shit was still the same too: same niggas on the block and same hood rats chasing behind them trying to trick for a few dollars. Only difference with them was that they looked like life had kicked their asses and they was tired as hell. Niggas had scars and faded tat-toos, while the hood rats had nasty stretch marks and fucked-up weaves and wigs. That's when I realized a nigga really ain't have shit left: money was gone, friends gone, wife gone, kids gone, house gone, cars gone.

"Hey, Breeze!" I heard a chick shout out as I got out of the car and headed up to my grand-ma's house.

I looked to my right to see a small-framed chick with a phat ass. *Goddamn!* I thought as my dick began to rise. I couldn't put a name to the face and the bitch wasn't even all that cute, but, I gotta say, after five years in the pen, that bitch was lookin' like Halle Berry and Salma Hayek rolled into one.

"What up, yo?" I said as I gave shorty a nod as soon as my moms was inside the house.

"You don't even know who I am. Do you?" she asked as she got a little closer.

"Nah, baby girl. You look familiar, but I can't call it." I was straight up with the chick.

"See how niggas do? Fuck and buck. You took my damn virginity in your grandmamma basement, nigga!" she snapped while playfully punching my arm.

"Oh, shit! Trixy?" I said, remembering that day like it was yesterday.

"Goddamn right. What up, fool?" She gave me a big hug.

"Ain't shit. Just happy to be home," I said sincerely.

"Oh, yeah? This your first stop?"

"Yep."

"What? Where your niggas at? Your wife? All your bitches? Before you got locked up you had a whole entourage. Where all them people at now? They suppose to be throwing you a welcome home party, greeting you with money, clothes, your favorite food and pussy all night." Trixy spoke like the true hood rat she was.

"Yeah, but you know how it go, money gone, niggas gone. Ain't nothing, though. A nigga a'ight," I lied. Deep inside I did want all that, and it was fucked up it didn't turn out that way, but I wasn't gonna let that petty shit break me.

"Well, welcome home, baby," Trixy said while hugging me tight.

Just the feeling of her titties against my chest was enough to make a nigga wanna bust, but I nonchalantly hugged her back and said, "A'ight, li'l momma, I'ma catch you later on."

No sooner than she'd turned around to walk away did the sight of her phat ass cause all the blood in my body to rush to my head, if you know what I mean. Just looking at this bitch's ass damn near made me dizzy. I grabbed her by the arm and pulled her close again, then whispered in her ear while I pulled her in for another hug. "Why don't you let me tap that for old time's sake? That would be a hell of a welcome home gift."

"Psssh! Nigga, please! First of all, that shit you just said is corny. Second, you ain't hitting shit because you ain't got shit. I ain't the same little naive girl I used to be when you popped my cherry. Shit done changed. I grew up, you sucka-ass nigga," Trixy snapped.

I didn't even respond. I just looked at this bitch like she was crazy.

"Yeah, that's right, nigga, you gotta get your weight up before you can even think about hitting this!" she said in response to my confused look.

"Oh, so it's like that?" I said, trying to register what the fuck just happened.

"Damn right it's like that," Trixy said as she walked away.

I was in silence as I walked through the gates of my grandma's yard. I had to wonder how a nothing-ass bitch like Trixy could diss me. That was my first realization that being at the bottom and staying straight wasn't gonna be easy.

"Now, there's my boy," my grandma shouted, causing me to divert my mind from Trixy.

I looked toward the house to see Grandma smiling. She rushed from the porch and hugged me tight. It was so good to see her. Throughout my bid, she and Moms were the only ones sending me holiday cards and sparing whatever they had to make sure a nigga had money on the books. That's how you know who your real peoples are.

"Grandma, it's been a long time," I replied.

"You got that right. I don't ever want to see you behind bars again. You hear me?" My grandma repeated the same phrase she had said to me so many times while I was locked up.

"I hear you now, and heard you every time you came to visit me," I assured her.

Being locked in a cage for five years, I couldn't do nothing but think about how my life had turned out. At least I could say that one good thing came out of me going to prison: a nigga got saved. I had this prison mate who would drill me every day about the Lord. That nigga talked about religion so much we started calling him Moses. Man, it was Moses who brought me through some of my roughest moments during my bid. It came to a point where I couldn't keep denying that nigga when he would tell me to come to the prison church with him. It took a little while, and a lot of rejections from me, but once he finally got me to start going, I really got into it. The more I learned about Jesus and the Bible, I began to realize that Jesus had a soldier's heart. He was real gangster. What other nigga you know would walk up in the gambling spot, flipping over tables and demanding respect? Only a true gangster would have the balls to do something like that.

Once I was baptized, Moses made me a necklace with a cross as a constant reminder of my newfound love for Christ. I hadn't taken it off since. Matter of fact, the night before I was re-

20255581

leased I couldn't sleep, so I said a little prayer. I made a personal vow to God that if He would just help me live right and get my family back, then I would stay away from the game and never ever return to prison again.

As I sat and chatted with my grandma, the house phone rang.

"Baby, it's for you." Ma pointed to me with the phone.

"Who is it?" I inquired, surprised. Hell, I hadn't even been home a whole hour. I wondered who would know that I had hit the bricks already.

"That mixed-breed bitch." My heart started pounding as I registered what my moms was saying. I didn't know whether to start cursing Maria's ass out for hanging me out to dry while I was locked up and keeping me away from my kids, or to let her know how much I loved and missed her. Truth was, I was mad at her for a couple of years after she cut off all communication with me, but as time passed, I really missed my wife and kids. When it came down to it, I loved the shit outta that bitch. Even with the news about her selling my house, I was still willing to get past all of it just to be with my family again.

"Talk nice to her so she will let you see the kids. It would be nice to see my grandbabies. Maria stopped coming around years ago," Moms whispered as she handed me the phone.

"Hello," I greeted her.

"Oh, so it is true. The almighty Breeze has been released from prison."

"You got a motherfucking nerve to be—" I began to shout before being cut off.

"Now, listen up, my soon-to-be ex-husband, I didn't call to get a sermon from you about how you feel. I called to let you know how things are going to be. I want to make a proposal to you," Maria offered.

"Yeah, I'm listening." I responded in a low tone because I didn't want her to hang up on me.

"These days, I know you're short on cash, so I'm willing to give you two thousand dollars to sign over your parental rights. My soon-to-be husband and I would like him to have custody of the kids. You and I both know who's been taking care of them all these years," she said.

My blood was boiling as I listened to her speak. "If you think I'm going to give up my rights—" I screamed before being cut off again.

"You're yelling. That's not something I'm willing to tolerate. Think about it and get back to me."

"Can I talk to my kids?" I asked calmly.

"No," Maria responded, and hung the phone up in my ear.

"No, this motherfucking bitch didn't just hang up the fucking phone on me!" I yelled. I checked the caller ID, but Maria had blocked it. I threw the cordless phone across the room. Lucky for Maria, she wasn't in front of me saying that shit. I would have grabbed her by the neck and squeezed every bit of life from her. I wanted to kick the wall in. One thing about Maria, she always knew how to get under my skin.

"Breeze, calm down, baby. You gon' make that little girl send you back to prison. Now I know you have plans to hit the streets celebrating with your friends or something. Why don't you do that? Have yourself a little fun, baby!" Grandma said, trying to lighten up my mood.

"Yeah, you're right, Grandma. I do have plans," I lied, then I directed my attention to my mother. "Ma, can I hold something until later?"

"Until later? Where you gonna get it from to get it to me later? All I have to give you is twenty, because money is tight around here and we need every dollar. Besides, if you had left some of your money with me instead of that money-hungry bitch, you wouldn't have this problem." My moms always seemed to find a way to tie Maria into every conversation.

"Chill, Ma, why you always gotta start talking a whole bunch of mess?" I questioned as I reached for the money. I felt like a thirteen-year-old begging his moms for allowance. I couldn't believe this was what my life had come down to. "Ladies, I will be back in a couple of hours." I kissed them both on the cheek, then I walked out of the house feeling like a bum-ass nigga.

My first thought was to go get some trees, but I knew I'd have to see my parole officer first thing the next morning. I had to settle for liquor instead. With that decided, I headed for the liquor store. While walking I was deep in thought. The conversation I'd just had with Maria kept playing in my head. *I can't believe this bitch tried to get me to sell my kids for two grand.* The thought of that shit pissed me off all over again.

"Breeze!" I heard somebody calling out my name. I was about to turn to see who it was, but then I kept walking when I realized this was the same fucking voice that had dissed me earlier.

"Nigga, I know you hear me calling you!" the voice shouted even louder.

I stopped in my tracks and turned around. "What the fuck do you want?"

"Calm down, hothead! I just wanted to apologize for what I said earlier," Trixy stated.

"Apologize for what? You say what you mean and you mean what you say, right?" I said, not giving much credit to her statement.

"Nah, I ain't mean to do you like that. It's just that niggas that ain't about nothing be coming at me all day saying dumb shit, so snapping off comes second nature to me. You feel me?" she said while she played with her hands and avoided making eye contact with me.

"A'ight shorty, everything good. I'm going down the block." I attempted to end the conversation.

"Damn, you just got home. You trying to stand on the corner with your niggas already?"

"What? Nah, I ain't on that shit right now. I'm just trying to clear my head right now. I'm headed to the liquor store."

"For real? Can you bring me back something?" Trixy asked.

"And me too," a little voice chimed in.

I looked to my right to see a little boy running up to Trixy. "Who's that, Momma?" he asked while pointing at me, then continued, "Is this my daddy or something?" He looked like a little gangster.

"Boy, get your little behind out of here!" Trixy commanded. "You need to stay out of grown folk's business! Didn't I tell you your daddy was in the Navy and that's why he's always gone? Now this here is Mr. Breeze. He is an old friend," Trixy explained.

"Well, why I ain't never seen you before?" the little runt asked me.

"I probably been in jail your whole life. How old are you, little nigga?" I asked.

"Six!" he said proudly, with his chest out.

"And what's your name?"

"Junior," he responded with a hint of attitude in his voice.

"A'ight, little man. I'll holla at you." I watched him as he walked off, heading toward the rec center. Little nigga had a confident swagger that reminded me of a younger me. I quickly shook my head to clear my thoughts, and turned back toward Trixy. "What you drinking?"

"Bacardi rum Bahama Mama the 1.75, liter bottle," she quoted like she worked for the ABC store or something.

"A'ight, I got you," I said as I continued to the store.

My thoughts went back to Junior as I walked away. I kind of felt bad for the little dude. I knew

Trixy probably had no fucking idea who his daddy really was. The crazy thing was how the little nigga kind of favored me. *Naw, couldn't be. That's all I need is a little soldier I don't know about,* I thought as I got closer to the store.

Once in the store I searched for Trixy's liquor. I grabbed it, then grabbed a small bottle of Hennessy and headed to the register.

"Twenty-eight dollars and thirty-two cents," the cashier stated.

Oh, shit! I ain't got but twenty dollars, I thought as I looked at the total on the register to confirm what I'd just heard. Embarrassed, I had to tell the cashier lady I only wanted the Bahama Mama. There was no way I could go back to the house without Trixy's drink. Minutes later I was near her crib.

"That was quick," she yelled as I walked up.

"Here you go. That's a big bottle for such a small lady." I handed Trixy her bottle.

"So what you get for yourself?" Trixy asked, noticing I was empty-handed.

"Nothing. I'm good," I lied. I didn't want to tell her how bad I really needed a drink but couldn't afford it.

"Nah, I can't drink alone. I'll be right back." Trixy disappeared through the barred storm door of her house. Moments later, she returned with a glass filled with ice and another glass filled with ice and a dark liquid. "Here. This is for you." She handed me the drink.

"What is it?" I asked as I sniffed the glass. My nostrils filled with a familiar scent.

"Hennessy."

Perfect, I thought as I took a big gulp. The Hennessy burned my throat all the way to my chest as it went down. It'd been so long since I had some liquor in my system, I could feel the shit coating my stomach and going into my veins. Trixy and I sat on the porch and chatted as we drank. Before I knew it, two hours had passed and we had talked about everything from old times to who's who in the present-day drug game. I was surprised at just how much she knew. It wasn't long after Trixy had taken the last swallow from her bottle that she began to get a little frisky. Somehow I knew it was coming.

"I know you didn't buy yourself anything because you didn't have enough money," she said in a drunken slur.

"Oh, yeah?" I said, taking another sip of my drink. Nigga was feeling real nice right about now.

"Yeah. If you didn't want anything you wouldn't have drunk all those glasses of Hennessy I brought you. It's cool, though. That's kinda sexy. You left your drink behind and bought mine." Trixy came really close to me, then whispered in my ear, "Just thinking about that shit turns me on." I could feel her lips on my ear, and the heat from her breath radiate down my neck.

Although everything in me wanted to grab her, lay her across the porch, rip off her clothes, and fuck the shit out of her, there was no way I was gonna give this girl another chance to diss me. So I looked at her out the corner of my eye, then turned my head like what she did had no effect on me at all.

"Just in case you didn't understand the message behind what I was saying, translation: my pussy is wet. You can't ignore this for long," Trixy said as she turned around, placed her ass directly in my face, then headed toward the front door.

It took everything in me not to pounce on that ass right away, but I knew I had to play it cool and make her wait a little bit. After about a minute flat, I couldn't hold out any longer and had to give in. Still refusing to run after her, I got up and took another thirty seconds to stroll toward where she was standing. As I got closer, she turned around, and I was immediately hypnotized by her booty. I found myself walking in a trance-like state right behind Trixy and that irresistible ass of hers.

"I thought you would see it my way." She smiled as she opened the door.

"Where's your son?" I asked, not wanting to be in the middle of fucking his mom from the back and have him run in on us.

"I sent him to my mom's crib for the night" Trixy said, then continued, "My place ain't much, but it will do for right now." She locked the door after I came in.

"This is cool," I responded, looking around.

Her crib was decent. Even though Trixy was kind of on the ghetto side, her taste was pretty close to that of my boogie-ass wife, Maria. Her place was set up almost the same way as the living room in my old house. She had a bad-ass cream couch and love seat that fit the room perfectly, and I was really digging the chocolate lounging chair. Not only that, but the bitch had a sixty-inch flat screen that really set it off. I must say, a nigga was impressed.

"I need to go to my bedroom for a minute. Please make yourself at home. I got Heineken chilling in the fridge if you wanna take the buzz off from all that Hennessy," Trixy offered.

I quickly went to the fridge and grabbed a bottle, hoping that shit really would take the buzz off. A nigga was really feeling drunk. Shortly after I sat down on the couch, music started playing. It was the sound of Trey Songz's "Neighbors Know My Name." I knew exactly what was coming next. I hadn't had any pussy in over five years, and I knew the slightest touch would cause me to bust within seconds. I wasn't about to take a chance at embarrassment. As a nigga, I already knew what I had to do.

"Trixy, where's your bathroom?" I yelled down the hall.

"It's the first door on the left," she yelled back.

I rushed to the bathroom and gently shut the door. I wasted no time pulling my pants down. I scanned the room quickly, and grabbed the first bottle of lotion I saw sitting on the counter. I poured some Victoria's Secret Japanese cherry blossom into my palm and started jerking off. Thinking of all those models in the *Hustler* magazine I kept while locked up made me cum pretty fast. I flushed the toilet to pretend like I actually used the bathroom, then cleaned myself up. Now I was ready for the real thing. I went back to the living room and sat on the couch. Minutes later, Trixy walked in, dressed in nothing but a sheer robe. My eyes were on the imprint of her ass and titties as she approached me. She stood directly in front of me, then propped one foot up on the couch beside me.

"Do you wanna know what I'm thinking?" she said in the most seductive way.

"What?" I asked, hoping that she was thinking she wanted to deep throat my dick. I was already rock hard just from the thought.

"I'm thinking . . ." Trixy came in closer to me then continued, "I'm thinking . . . Why would you smell like Victoria's Secret?" she said, totally throwing off the moment.

"Oh, after I washed my hands I needed a little lotion. Now get back to what you were about to say before you smelled the lotion." I slid my hand beneath her robe and rubbed her thigh.

"I was thinking about the first time we had sex. I was a little girl back then. Well, I'm a grown woman now, with big-girl moves," Trixy said as she parted open her robe and mounted her right leg on the couch's arm, exposing her thick, pink pussy. I don't know if it's because it was the first pussy I'd seen in years, but I swear she had the prettiest set of lips I'd ever seen in my life! She slid her hand between her legs and began to massage her pussy. "I'm going to fuck the shit out of you." She dropped her robe completely, then continued, "Come get this pussy, baby."

I leaned forward and guided my right hand from her thigh up to her right breast. Next, I squeezed her nipple while I played with her clit and watched my fingers disappear into her cave. She licked my fingers, which were dripping from her wetness.

"Take your pants off," she instructed as she got on her knees in between my legs. I pulled my pants down as fast as humanly possible, and she wasted no time putting it in her mouth. She started off sucking my dick and licking the tip just the way I liked it. My eyes started rolling in the back of my head. I was so into it that I didn't even realize that she'd used her lips to put a condom on me. *Damn, this bitch is a magician,* I thought, amazed that she was able to do that without me even feeling it. Her mouth felt so warm and tender as she bobbed her head up and down my shit. I could feel my dick twitch as she glided her tounge in swirls and tightened her cheeks with every head stroke. The way she was doing that shit, it felt like I was in a pussy for real. *Goddamn!* I said to myself that she wasn't lying when she said she was a big girl, 'cause this chick was sucking like a professional!

"Suck that shit, Trixy," I commanded her, while doing all I could to prevent myself from cumming. I didn't want to cum in her mouth. Not this round anyway. I wanted to cum inside her, instead. After a couple of minutes, I bent her over and put her into a position on all fours. I held on to her titties as I fucked her from behind. After all these years, her pussy was still nice and tight, and her shit was soaking wet, just how I liked it.

"Fuck me harder," she ordered. She was taking every long stoke I was giving her and loving it. We switched positions and she ended up on top, straddling me. Trixy rode me as if I were the last nigga on earth with a dick. *Damn, this girl got some good pussy*, I thought as I grabbed her waist tight and forced all nine inches of myself deep inside her. Trixy switched positions again, and her lips landed back on my dick. She pulled off the condom. She sucked it even harder this time. The warmth and wetness from her mouth made me cum within seconds. When I came, she let it shoot all over her face. Trixy was a real freak. We fucked three times within four hours and she still wanted more. But fuck that, I was done. Fucking with Trixy, I would end up missing my appointment with my parole officer. This girl was on a mission, and she definitely proved to me she was all grown up now.

The chirping sound of the alarm clock woke me at seven o'clock in the morning. That shit was like music to my ears. I preferred that any day over the sound of a prison guard shouting at me, "Motherfucker, get the hell up! Chow time." When I got home after that long night with Trixy, I made sure I set the alarm so I didn't miss my first appointment with my parole officer. I hopped out of the bed and headed to the bathroom. As I brushed my teeth, bacon and eggs began lingering in the air. After putting on my clothes, last night came to mind. *Damn, that pussy was good. Trixy wore my ass out. She's definitely not a virgin anymore.* I knew from that day I was going to continue to get into that tight little cave on a regular basis. Even though I had a hell of a time with Trixy the night before, I still couldn't get my wife off my mind. My face instantly frowned up, and my heart started to pound when I thought about what that bitch had said to me about giving up my parental rights so she could let another nigga raise my kids. *I'll be dead before I have some next nigga playing Daddy to my kids*. I felt the rage start to build up inside me, so I had to stop myself and get back on track. I looked in the mirror as I spoke to myself, "Today is a brand new beginning for me. I'm at my crossroads and will go the right way. I will not let bitches, money, or the streets bring me down. The meeting with my parole officer is top priority today."

After getting my thoughts and priorities back on track, I headed to the kitchen, where my moms was hard at work cooking breakfast.

"Morning, Ma," I greeted her, with a kiss on the cheek. She had made a feast for me. My favorite meal of the day had always been breakfast.

"Hey, baby, how did you sleep last night?" she asked with one hand turning over frying bacon and the other holding a cigarette.

"Pretty good."

"Let me fix you a plate to get your day started off right," she offered.

"Thanks, Ma. Before I went in, you promised me you would stop smoking," I reminded her.

"With stress from my job, bills, and you locked up, I needed something to help me cope. I'll tell you what, Breeze. If you can go out there and get a job, I'll quit smoking cold turkey," she vowed while laying my plate on the kitchen table in front of me.

"It's a deal," I agreed. While I ate, I tried not to think about Maria's conniving ass, but the bitch kept popping back up. *This chick won't even let me see my own damn kids.* Every time I thought about her, my head started hurting.

I rushed and finished my food, then headed out the door. I wanted to make sure I was at least thirty minutes early for my appointment. I thought that would impress my parole officer. From what I'd heard, a P.O. could make or break you, and I damn sure didn't need anyone else going against me. My odds of survival were bad enough already. Once I was on the bus, I decided I would relax on the way there and have my daily conversation with my main man upstairs. I figured if I put it in his hands, I'd be okay. I put my hand on the cross hanging off the necklace Moses had given me, and closed my eyes.

"Byron Miller," a man called out as I waited in the foyer. Once I got up, he led me to his office. I didn't know what to expect.

"Your name is Byron Miller?" he questioned.

"Yeah." I nodded.

"Well, son, my name is Winston Hicks and I'm going to be your parole officer," he explained while pulling out a cup from his desk drawer.

"What's that for?" I asked.

"This cup is for you to piss in. You get one of these tests once a month. You fuck up once and you go straight back to jail. First and foremost, I don't put up with no bullshit. This morning I reviewed your record. I must say it was quite long. If you're a smart man, for your sake, I hope you put all that shit behind you and have plans to change your street ways. By the way, whatever your dumb-ass street name is, I won't call you that. Your name is Byron Miller to me. Here are some job sites I need you to go on, and I will follow up with these employers. If you don't go, you've won yourself a one-way ticket to jail. As I said before, I don't play no games. Now, if you really want to better yourself, I will help you as much as I can. You got that, son?"

"Yes, sir." I nodded again.

"Now, don't waste my time. Go on and do that piss test. The bathroom is on the right," he instructed while handing me the cup. Thankfully, I hadn't smoked.

After the test results came out negative, I was able to take the next step and start looking for a job. Hicks gave me a long list that would take me at least two days to finish, so I dove right into it. I was stepping out of Farm Fresh, where I applied for a night stocker position, when some of my old boys drove by. I didn't have shit, but I wasn't going to let them see me sweat.

"Breezy, Breeze," I heard a call from the car. I walked up to them.

"What up, nigga." They each dapped me up. They were eager to see what was going on with me.

"I'm good." I nodded.

"What you got going on for the rest of the day?" Mannie asked.

"My schedule is all open. What's good?" I replied.

"Say no more. Hop in," he offered. I jumped in and Mannie sped off.

For the next two hours, I rode around with my niggas while they made their rounds doing pickups. It reminded me of my days in the game, riding around, checking niggas on the block and collecting my dough. Yeah, being with those niggas made me miss the game for a split second, but when I thought about those five years and the vow I'd made the night before my release, I ain't give a fuck about the game. My boys told me what had been up since I'd been gone. They passed the blunt around as we chatted. I declined the blunt but welcomed the information about the streets. I saw this as a perfect opportunity to verify the information I had gotten from Trixy. I asked about some of the dudes I used to roll with: Killa Mike, Cash, and Peady.

Mannie quickly gave me the rundown. "Mike and Cash got shot up during a robbery. These niggas was dressing up like the police and robbing trap houses. It didn't take long for niggas to catch on. So one night, when these niggas tried to hit a crib, niggas was waiting on them. As soon as they kicked the door in, niggas sprayed their ass. Killa got hit fifteen times, so he ain't make it, and Cash caught five. That nigga made it, but he paralyzed, shitting and pissing on his self every day. From what I hear, Peady supposed to be doing it big down south somewhere."

None of that shit Mannie said was really a surprise to me. Since Mike and Cash had snitched on me, I knew those grimey niggas had it coming. As far as Peady, he was my right-hand man, so he knew how the game went. Not only did he have my knowledge about how to get things done, but he ran off with my money, so why wouldn't he be doing good? Mannie went on to say that a nigga named Mr. Biggs was like Wal-Mart, and everyone in the seven cities was buying from him.

"I'm holding shit down in Norfolk. Whenever you ready, nigga, I can put you back on," Mannie offered.

"Nah, duke. I ain't fucking with that." I declined his offer just as easily as I had declined the blunt earlier.

"All right, Breeze. I hear you, man. You trying to be on that good-boy shit. Every nigga like that when they first hit the bricks, but you know that shit'll wear off after a while. Once the streets whip that ass real good, you'll go back to what you know. And it's this motherfucking white girl you know best, nigga!" Mannie spoke the truth.

Deep down, I knew what Mannie was saying was right. Selling drugs and making street paper were just about the only things I was really good at. I knew it wasn't gonna be a easy task, but I owed it to my kids, Ma, and my grandma to stay on the right path and live legit this time around. I had expected getting propositions from niggas, so I already had my head straight. A weak nigga would have easily given in. Before the ride was over, each of them hit me off with a few dollars.

I had them drop me off at an old building a few blocks from my grandma's crib. There was a job there I needed to check out.

"I'm here about the janitorial position you got," I said as I walked in the front door.

There was a bald-headed black man sitting at a desk, reading the newspaper. He didn't even look up as he spoke to me. "You got any experience son?"

"Nah, man. I'm just looking for a gig. I know how to clean up, but I ain't never had no job," I said, being honest.

I didn't know what it was about this man, but I just felt like he was from the streets. He reminded me of an O.G. He finally put down his newspaper and looked up at me. He was silent as he looked me up and down from head to toe. "You on parole, boy?"

"Yes, sir," I answered. There wasn't any sense in lying. I figured my parole officer had already given him a heads-up that I'd be coming by, anyway.

"What you do time for? Drugs?" he asked like he knew me or something.

"Yes, sir."

"You doing this to keep your P.O. off your back or you really trying to change?" The O.G. asked question after question.

"Man, I'm trying to live right. I lost a whole lot during that five-year bid. I'm just trying to build my life back and do it the right way," I said sincerely.

"Okay, my man. I've been in your shoes. You remind me of myself when I first got out the pen. I'm gonna give you a try, but one fuck up and you're out the door. Can you start tonight?"

"Yes, sir! I can start right now if you need me to!" I quickly took the O.G. up on his offer.

"Okay. Meet me at Freedom Bank on Granby Street at seven o'clock. If you're late, you're fired," he said as he laid down the rules. "Dress comfortably."

"I'll be there. Thanks, man," I said, then walked back out of the office.

I rushed home full of excitement. I wasn't excited about being a janitor, considering I used to have a maid of my own. To tell you the truth, the shit was kind of depressing. But I knew this was one step in the right direction and one step closer to getting my kids back.

I had just enough time to get some lunch and take a nap. While I was coming in the door, Ma and Grandma were watching the news. Ma was standing by the couch looking as if she'd just come home from work, and Grandma was in her recliner, munching on some salted peanuts.

"Hey, Breeze, how did your day go?" Ma eagerly asked.

"It was a'ight. I saw my P.O. and I got a li'l gig," I announced, nodding my head.

"That's wonderful. Where is the job?" Grandma inquired after taking her glasses off.

"It's at Freedom Bank on Granby Street. I'm going to be a janitor working the evening shifts," I explained.

"When do you start?" Ma questioned.

"Tonight."

"Breeze, I'm so proud of you. Come give this old lady a hug," Grandma replied, reaching her arms toward me. "I know it's not the best job in the world, and it's not gonna be easy, but at least it will keep you off the streets."

"Yeah, and now you can start helping out with the bills!" Ma chimed in.

"Don't worry about me. I'll do my part. Now are you gonna do your part and stop smoking?" I reminded Ma about the deal she'd previously made.

"Oh, shit, Breeze, I forgot all about our deal. Okay, I'll try my best . . . right after this pack is finished! This shit cost me almost ten dollars and I'm not about to throw them away!" She chuckled.

"Yeah, a'ight, Ma," I said, knowing my mom was full of shit.

"Let me fix you something to snack on. We are about to fry some fish," Grandma suggested as she got up from her La-Z-Boy chair.

After eating dinner, I took a nap, and awoke to the sounds of gunshots. I looked out the window to see a nigga lying in the street and a car speeding off. It looked like a drive-by. Just another reminder I was back in the fucking hood. I glanced at the clock and saw it was already six. I hopped up, threw on my clothes, and headed out the door. I'd never had a job before in my life and I'd never wanted one. Who ever thought Breezy Breeze would be working, and as a janitor? Boy, shit had really changed.

I showed up at the bank fifteen minutes early. The O.G. was just pulling up. I saw this fine-ass chick standing by the front enterance as I was walking up to the bank. She had a dark-skinned, amaretto complexion, and was about five feet six, with long, thick black hair. I could tell her shit wasn't no weave, either. Her ass was nice and thick, shaped like an upside-down heart. She didn't have much to her breasts but I could tell they were just big enough to grab and squeeze. She was definitely the "take home to momma" type. I watched as she was locking up the place.

"Hold that door, baby girl," the O.G. hollered as he rushed up.

"Grab some of these things, son." He handed me a bucket of cleaning supplies. I grabbed them and followed him in.

Knowing I wasn't in any position to holla at any respectable-type chick, a girl like her, I didn't even look in her direction as we walked in.

"Good evening," I heard a soft voice say. I was surprised that she'd acknowledged me.

"How you doing?" I tried to sound polite and gentlemen-like.

"Very good, thank you. Have a good night," she said as she walked away.

"You too." I nodded.

A nigga was feeling real low right about now. Before I'd gotten locked up, I could pull any girl I wanted, because my game was always tight. No woman could deny me: black, white, hood, rich, whatever they were, they loved them some Breezy Breeze. I had all the accessories to go along with my good looks and irresistible charm, too. The money, clothes, jewels, and cars. There was no way I could come at this bank lady, broke, fresh out of jail, and working a janitorial job. What real bitch would want a nigga like that? I really had to do something about my situation.

"Son, getting here on time is half the battle. Now let's get to work," the O.G. said while taking the cleaning supplies I was holding and handing me a dust vacuum.

"You know how to use that?" he asked.

"Yes, sir," I lied. I'd never used one, but I knew I could figure it out.

"Well, get to work!"

This gig was a piece of cake. The rules were simple. Anything left on the desk, I couldn't dare touch. I had to make sure the trash was emptied every night, vacuum, and dust. I had to clean up the bathrooms and break rooms, sweep and mop if there was a spill. There was no way I could fuck that up!

Chapter 2

All in a Day's Work
Tanisha

Clients can really stress me out, but Mr. Biggs and his wife earned the grand prize. Mr. Biggs was one of the bank's biggest clients, as well as one of my biggest headaches. As soon as I saw him coming off the elevator, I took a fast detour into my office, quickly picked up the phone, and put it to my ear. I pulled up my computer screen and pretended to be deep in conversation with whomever was on the phone. Even though I put on an Oscar-winning performance, Mr. Biggs still rudely walked into my office and interrupted me.

"Ms. Johnson, may I speak with you for a moment?" He stood in front of my desk.

I held up one finger to signal that I'd be with him in a minute, as I wrapped up my bogus phone conversation.

"What can I do for you today, Mr. Biggs?" I tugged at my skirt as I stood up, in an attempt to lengthen it a bit.

"There are quite a few things that come to mind," Mr. Biggs said while walking toward me. He grabbed my hand, then whispered in my ear, "When are you gonna stop playing hard to get? A little Southern beauty like you should be getting spoiled, not working hard every day as some little old bank branch manager."

My stomach turned as I felt the heat from Mr. Biggs's breath on my forehead. That sensation along with the combined scent of Doublemint gum and Prada cologne really made me want to vomit.

"Daddy, Daddy." Mr. Biggs's moment of sexual harassment was interrupted by his kids running into my office.

"Hey, Jaden. Hi, Kaylyn!" I happily greeted them.

"Hi, Ms. Johnson!" They rushed into my arms, greeting me with big hugs.

"What's going on in here?" Maria walked in with the same rude demeanor she had on a daily basis. I couldn't figure out if she was just a miserable person or if she had a personal vendetta against me.

"Nothing, sweetheart, just discussing some last-minute business transactions with Ms. Johnson," Mr. Biggs lied.

"Looks like a little more than talking was going on from where I was standing," Maria said, eyeing Mr. Biggs. Then she directed her attention to me. "Are you hard of hearing, darling? Otherwise I don't understand why you must be so close to my man when he's speaking to you."

More like your man is all up on me, bitch, I said in my head, but wouldn't dare let that type of language come out of my mouth. I was much too classy to stoop to Maria's level. I chose to ignore her comment, and turned toward Mr. Biggs. "Is there anything else you need today, Mr. Biggs? Was everything taken care of for you" I asked.

"Everything is fine, Ms. Johnson," he replied. "As ususal," he leaned in and whispered to me when he noticed Maria was distracted with Kaylyn.

"Well, let's head to dinner. I've got reservations for us downtown. Come on, kids," Maria snapped, getting back to Mr. Biggs and me.

"Bye, Ms. Johnson!" the kids said in unison.

"Wait a minute. Don't forget your candy. You know Ms. Johnson always gives you candy." The kids rushed over to get their lollipops.

"After dinner." Maria snatched the candy from the kids' hands and they all headed out the door.

I was happy to see Mr. Biggs and Maria leave, but each time I saw those little rug rats they grew on me more and more. They were the only pleasurable part of Mr. Biggs and Maria's weekly visits. It was sad they had such a horrible person as a mother. It's against everything I know as a Christian to talk about people, but, truth be told, I didn't have anything nice to say about that woman. It took everything in me not to curse her out each time Maria's snobbish behind walked in the bank, with her nose in the air looking down on everybody like she's better than us. It's only by God's grace that her kids hadn't turned out like her. They're so cute and well mannered. I always looked forward to seeing them every week.

It was obvious Maria didn't like me, but I guess when your man is always with another woman, you would have to be on the defensive. On the other hand, if the cheating was that bad for Maria, she could have left him a long time ago. Rumor had it, Jaden and Kaylyn weren't Mr. Biggs's kids anyway, so she could easily have left without any ties. I guess to some women, money was all worth it. It was customary for Mr. Biggs to flirt and make passes at women in the bank while Maria wasn't looking, or especially if she wasn't around, but sometimes he was bold enough to do it practically right in front of her. He's the kind of man who just won't take no for an answer.

My secretary buzzed not even five minutes after Mr. Biggs and Maria had walked out of my office. "Ms. Johnson, the tellers need you up front."

"Mrs. Biggs, unfortunately, our shipment is running late. I won't have those brand new hundreds for you for the next hour. As an alternative, I can get you brand new fifty dollar bills," I heard my lead teller say as I walked up.

"I've been coming in the branch every week at 4:00 p.m. with the same request. This isn't anything new. I want my hundreds. And I want them now," Maria demanded as she looked me up and down while clenching her Chanel purse.

For the next ten minutes, she gave me a lecture about how much she and Mr. Biggs had invested with the bank, as though they were our only big clients. Believe me, we had other clients with much more than Mr. Biggs. As my temples tightened, I decided to call another branch. Fortunately, they had those precious brand new hundreds Maria so desperately needed.

"I'm going to have to go to another branch to get the money for you, Maria. It will take me about thirty minutes. Is that okay?" I asked, hoping she would decline my offer since she had dinner plans.

"You're ruining my dinner plans, but I will wait. I'm sending you to teach you a lesson. I'm sure the next time you will be prepared," Maria barked.

I didn't respond as I walked out of the bank. My assistant manager and I drove to the other branch. When we returned, Maria made me personally count each bill into her hand. I developed a terrible migraine from the fiasco, and decided to go home. I quickly straightened my desk and packed up my things, then headed out the door.

"Smile, baby girl. It can't be that bad." I looked up to see a familiar face. I instantly recognized the little cutie I'd met the night before. He was passing by as I was heading out the door.

"Yes, it is." I nodded smiling.

"Aw. You need a hug, sweetheart?" The cleaning guy smiled, showing his perfect pearly whites.

"I need a hug, foot rub, and an Excedrin," I vented.

"Don't you have a man to do all that for you?" he asked right away.

"I don't see how that's any of your business. But if you must know, yes, I do have a man," I replied, even though I was lying through my teeth. I was not about to admit how alone and desperately single I really was. Shoot, I wished I did have a man to go home to on tiring days like today.

"I know you're lying, but it's cool." He smirked, "I can afford to give you that hug now, but I'm gonna have to owe you that foot rub."

"Nothing is this world is free. What are you going to expect in return?" I quickly responded, knowing the business of give and take.

"You won't owe me anything. You've already paid me with your smile. I really needed to have a beautiful woman smile at me today, so you can say we'll be even. Your smile will carry until to-morrow. Problem is, what am I gonna do when I need my next fix?" He gave me a mischievous smile, then continued, "I'm gonna need to see you every morning for that."

"And how do you plan on making that hap-pen?" I asked, curious to hear how this guy would respond. His words were so corny, but his swagger was adorable.

"Well, I was thinking. You could give me your number. Then give me your address. Then I'll stop by every morning, give you a call, and tell you I'm outside. Then you could just stick your head out the window and smile." We both burst out in laughter. This guy was hilarious!

"I can't give you my address, but I will take your number." Although I knew deep inside that I had no intention of calling this guy, there was no way I could tell him no. He was so sweet and charming. After all, he did put a smile on my face.

"Okay. What's the number?" I pulled out my BlackBerry Curve, and entered his number as he called out each digit.

"What's your name, baby girl?" he asked.

"Tanisha. And yours?"

"Breeze."

"Breeze?" I giggled. I could only imagine where such a name came from.

"Yep," he said proudly, like he wasn't ashamed to have such a foolish nickname.

"Okay, Breeze. You have a good evening." I wrapped up our conversation.

"You do the same," he replied.

After a few steps, I heard a call. "Yo, Tanisha!"

I turned around to see Breeze standing with his arms wide open. "You forgot your hug!"

Although it was tempting, I didn't go around hugging perfect strangers, so I politely declined. "Thanks for the offer, but I'll be fine. Maybe next time."

Chapter 3

Apple of My Eye
Mr. Biggs

Of course my princess, Maria, is worthy of a man's faithful love, but I am such a great man that I feel it is only fair to spread myself around. So that's why every time I visit the bank, I make sure to give all the ladies a little taste. Sure, it is fun flirting with the different women there, but there is one of them in particular I have my heart set on, and that is Tanisha. Her innocence, professionalism, and extreme patience turn me on. Not only that, the woman is sexy as hell. She has a perfectly round booty with a cute little waist and thick thighs, and her breasts are the perfect size for me. I could close my eyes and feel my big, strong hands gripping those beautiful globes. Sometimes it even irritates me when Maria gives her a hard time. I think deep down inside Maria knows I have a thing for Tanisha. Hell, I am a man who believes you can have as many women as you can afford. Looking at my bank account, I can afford a whole army of women.

I've always been a ladies' man. I come from a long line of pimps and players. All of my uncles have plenty of money and women, and even my brothers do too. I guess I followed in their footsteps when it comes to the women, but instead of beating them, and mistreating them I am always more of the charmer. My oldest brother was one of the biggest dope dealers in Baltimore when we were younger. He had so many women he didn't know what do with them. Hell, it was one of his women I lost my virginity to. I came home from school on my sixteenth birthday and walked in my bedroom to find one of his girls on my bed, ass naked with her legs cocked open. "Happy Birthday," she sang as soon as I opened the door. I remember it like it was yesterday.

Although I love the ladies and love spoiling them even more, I demand loyalty and respect. I am sure to keep my woman in line, but I do it using the correct means.

"Was that really necessary, honey?" I asked Maria as we drove toward the oceanfront. Since she insisted on waiting for new hundred-dollar bills, we'd missed our dinner reservations downtown, so I had to make new ones near the oceanfront.

"Of course it was. They have got to learn to be prepared for my arrival," Maria said, as if the world stopped for her.

The sound of my ringing phone interrupted our conversation.

"Biggs," I answered.

"Sorry to bother you. I know this is usually your dinner time with the family, but I got a little piece of information you may want to know," Mannie said.

"Yeah? And what is that?" I wondered what the hell could be so important that Mannie had to call me outside of working hours. All my men knew I had certain hours of operation. Unless there was an emergency, no one was to call me outside of my working hours. I know the streets never close, but, through the years, I had put in enough time and dedication, and now I had my top soldiers to run my business so I could afford to set my hours.

"Breeze is home."

I was silent as I took in this bit of information. I'd hoped that I would receive that information from Maria and not off the streets. Now I had to wonder what she had to hide.

"A'ight. Keep watch and let me know what's up," I said, then hung up the phone.

"Maria." I glanced over at her sitting comfortably in the passenger seat of my BMW 750.

"Yes?"

"Is there anything you want to tell me?" I asked, giving her the opportunity to tell me about her husband's release.

"What do you mean, Biggs? Is there something you would like to know?" Maria said, full of attitude.

"This is not the time to sass me, woman," I said firmly to let her know I was serious.

"Well, I don't know what you're talking about."

"You think you should have told me about your husband being home?" I said calmly as we pulled up to the restaurant.

"No, because that's very insignificant. But if you must know, he is home and I have talked to him. I simply told him me and the kids have moved on, and that I want him to give up his parental rights so that you may raise them. I laid down the facts," Maria said, then looked in the mirror and applied her lip gloss.

"That's my baby girl. Keep Daddy happy. Next time just make sure you keep Daddy informed. I don't want to hear shit off the streets. I want to hear it from my woman. You understand?" I was proud Maria did what she'd planned for years, but, at the same time, I had to let her know that nothing happened without me knowing about it first. Now that that was discussed and over with, it was time for some good old Atlantic Ocean seafood. Maria, the kids, and I, pulled up to valet parking, hopped out of the car, and headed into the restaurant.

Chapter 4

Time For a Change
Breeze

"Here you go, son," the boss man said as he handed me my very first check.

"Goddamn, man. It's about time," I mumbled as I reached out for my pay. I hurried to open my check.

I was finally getting some money of my own. My hourly wage was ten dollars. I had worked forty hours a week for the past two weeks without getting paid yet. Apparently, we got paid weekly, but they hold on to your first week's check when you start a new job. I am not used to having to wait for my money like that. After I involuntarily donated to somebody name FICA, Medicare, and the state of Virginia, I barely had enough to buy a pair of Gucci sneakers. At this point Gucci, Louis, Prada, and all the fine things

58 Chunichi

I was used to were all mere memories. I might as well have been working for free. For the first time in my life I understood what Ma meant when I would hear her say, "I work my behind off every day tryin'a make a dollar, but instead I get paid in nickels and dimes." Not to mention, I would have to pay a fee to cash this little-ass check when I took it to the check cashing spot. Nevertheless, I took my check and rolled with it. Even though I personally couldn't do much with that little money, it was enough for me to grab a few things for my kids. I strolled through Lynnhaven Mall to see what kind of stuff I could pick up for them.

"My little nigga is gonna love these," I said to the cashier before handing her the money for the new Jordans I'd just purchased for my son. These shits were hot. I just hoped I had copped the right size for him. I hadn't seen him in years, but Ma had his size from the last time the "mixed-breed bitch" let her see her grandkids, so I bought it the next size up.

After leaving Kids Foot Locker, I visited the toy store and grabbed a few dolls for my Kaylen. Then I stopped by the cell phone booth and purchased a cheap little Boost Mobile. I wasted no time calling Maria.

"Hello?" she answered right away.

"What up, Maria?"

"How did you get my number?" she questioned.

"I could say fate. You know God don't like ugly. Or maybe you shouldn't put your shit in your pocket without locking it." I tried my best to stay calm while speaking to her.

"Okay, whatever. So are you calling to take me up on my offer?" Maria said in a condescending tone.

I wanted to say, "Fuck no," but instead I laughed and said, "Are you serious? You want me to let a next nigga raise my kids? You really expect me to sign over my rights for some two thousand dollars, Maria? I've lost a lot of things but I refuse to lose my kids. I ain't have no control over the other things I've lost, but I can do something about this shit. I'll do whatever it takes, Maria. Even if that means I have to drag your ass to court."

"First of all, in order to do that you would need to hire an attorney, which requires money, which you don't have. So what are you going to do, Breeze, get a court-appointed attorney? You would never win! Ha, ha, ha, ha!" Maria laughed in my ear like she took me for a fucking joke.

"Oh, so I'm a fucking joke now? What's a joke to you is death to me." I tried hinting to Maria my kids were serious shit to me.

"Is that a fucking threat, Breeze?" Maria yelled.

"Take it how you wanna take it. All I'm saying is I gave you all I had. I loved you and gave you everything you ever wanted or asked me for. I busted my ass to make you happy, Maria. You can't tell me you don't remember none of that. It's always been all about you, even when you turned your back on me while I was in prison. None of that shit matters now. If you have ever loved me, even in the least bit, I'm begging you, please; just let me see my kids," I pleaded.

Fortunately, after all that arguing and begging, Maria agreed to let me see my kids at Mount Trashmore. I can't lie, that shit made my day. To see my kids again made the two weeks of slaving and cleaning well worth it. I couldn't wait to get to the park to hug my children tight, and see how much they'd grown and what they looked like.

I arrived at the park thirty minutes early, anxiously anticipating the arrival of my children.

My heart pounded as I saw Maria and the kids walking toward me. My mind was racing. *Will my kids remember me? Do they even know I'm their father? And what about Maria . . . How am I suppose to deal with her?*

"All right, let's get this over with. I have a spa appointment and I can't be late," Maria said as soon as she walked up.

"Wow! After over three years without contact—no visit, no phone call, not even a letter—that's the first thing you say to me? How about 'how you been, nice to see you,' or something?" I screwed my face up and shook my head at Maria's evil ass.

"Whatever. What would be nice is getting a full body massage, facial, and body wrap instead of me wasting my time with you. I don't even know why I agreed to come here. But since I'm here, you have thirty minutes with the kids." She was sure to make it clear she'd rather be doing other things than be here with me.

Ignoring Maria's comments, I directed my attention toward my children.

"Man, y'all are so grown up." I greeted them with hugs.

A cold chill went down my spine as my kids turned back to look at Maria to make sure it was okay to hug their own damn father. I was their own flesh and blood, not that Mr. Biggs nigga. Putting my anger aside, I didn't hesitate to pull out the stuff I bought for them.

"The kids won't like these things. You should have asked me before buying . . . Excuse me, you probably stole it. You know you're broke. They're into Nintendo Wiis, DS games, and PlayStation 3," Maria stated.

After that bitch opened her mouth, I was afraid the kids wouldn't want what I bought, but, to my surprise, they did love their gifts.

"Wow! Jordans! My friend Nicolas has all the Jordans but Mom wouldn't buy me any. She said they were for ghetto kids. I told you they were cool, Mom!" Jaden said full of excitement. That put a permanent smile on my face. At that very moment, I felt like I was on top of the world.

With time ticking, I quickly took the kids over to the play area and played with them for a while. Just when we were really bonding and having fun, Maria brought her ass over tapping her diamond-faced Rolex watch.

"Your time is up," she shouted.

"Okay, kids. Time for you to go. Daddy will see you later," I followed the guidelines Maria set, in hopes that she will allow me to continue to visit with my children on a regular basis.

"Where are you living now? How will I be able to reach my kids?" I pleaded with my wife.

"You have a number for me. What more do you need?"

"Yeah, but you won't answer, Maria. I had to call for days before you picked up. Can I buy the kids a cell phone at least? I just want to be able to speak to them on a daily basis and see them at least once a week." I pleaded with my wife from hell.

Maria refused to give me any contact information, and refused to allow the kids to have a cell phone. I had to wonder, *What the fuck did I do to make this woman hate me so much?* I no longer put up a fight. I just let Maria have her way, and ended the argument. In order to speak to my children, I would call her every day a hundred times a day if I had to.

I gave my children a final hug, and watched as they walked away with their mother. A sudden sadness fell over me as I realized I didn't know when I would see my kids again. Maria had truly turned into a coldhearted bitch. Had she always been like this and I never noticed? I didn't understand how this could be the same woman I had fallen in love with. Damn, maybe I *had* been blinded by love back in the day. Either that or her nice attitude had been bought with my money. Then it dawned on me that maybe she'd always been this way and I was too caught up with my own shit to notice it.

After leaving the park I headed home. I'd had a long day and I was tired.

"My baby got his first real paycheck today," Ma announced as soon as I walked in the house.

Damn, I should have never told her when I was getting paid, because I knew she would be looking for a handout, I thought as I attempted to walk past her and head to my bedroom.

"The electric bill needs to get paid today, Breeze. You can go pay it at the nearest grocery store," she urged, handing me a piece of paper with the account number jotted down on it.

"Ma, I spent all of my money," I admitted.

"On what? I hope it wasn't for that mixed-breed bitch."

"No, I bought a few things for the kids. Before I knew it, the money was spent."

"Breeze, that was rightly dignified, but where you rest your head at needs some help too. Damn it, I was counting on you to pay this bill for me," Ma explained while pulling out a cigarette, then rubbing her temples.

"Ain't nothing, Ma. I got you on the next check," I simply replied.

"The bill is due now. I understand you wanted to do for your kids, but, shit, you could have brought home a gallon of milk or something. I mean, you ain't even pay me back that fucking twenty dollars I loaned you from the day you came home!" my ma said, full of frustration.

Ma sure knew how to make a nigga feel like less of a man. Not wanting to disrespect her, all I could do was hold my tongue and get the fuck out of dodge. Without saying a word, I rushed out of the house, slamming the door behind me.

No sooner had I slammed it, my ma flung it back open. "And don't be slamming my damn door! When you start paying some bills around here, then you can do whatever the fuck you like! Until then respect my shit," she yelled from the front porch.

"Yeah, a'ight, Ma," I said, and headed over to Trixy's crib.

"Trixy, open up," I urged as I banged on her front door.

"What's up," she asked through the crack in the door. She was dressed in a worn green robe with her hair wrapped up in an old oily scarf.

"I need a place to stay for a little while," I explained.

"Breeze, I don't know about that. Shit, I ain't even heard from you since we fucked over a week ago."

"I'm sorry, baby girl. A nigga got a little gig so I been working. Plus I just got a cell phone today. Come on, ma, you know you want this dick on a daily basis. What's better than waking up to it every morning?" I kicked my best game to Trixy.

"Yeah, the sex was great, but dick doesn't pay the bills. I can hardly care for me and my son. I damn sure can't afford to carry a nigga. You plan on helping me with some shit around here? Besides, weren't you staying with your moms rent free?"

"Yeah, but when my dick is hard at night I can't roll over on my momma. For the past week all a nigga been thinking about is what it would be like to hit that good pussy every night." I slid my hand into her robe, and whispered in her ear, "Now put that pussy on my fingers 'cause I know you're wet. Don't even act like the thought of that doesn't turn you on."

"A'ight, nigga, I tell you what. We'll try this living arrangement out for a few days. Then we'll see where it goes from there." Trixy agreed like I knew she would. All women try to come off hard, but with the right words, affection, and charm, a man is able to make them change their mind.

"You may as well say a few years, 'cause based on how you was acting the other night when I was in that, you ain't gon' ever let this dick walk out the door." I said sarcastically.

"Whatever, nigga." We both laughed as Trixy swung the door open for me to enter.

I rushed in and grabbed Trixy tight around the waist. "Daddy's home." We continued to laugh.

"And Daddy better get his shit together," Trixy quickly snapped back.

"Where's Junior?" I asked, wanting to make sure the coast was clear.

"The Boys & Girls Club."

"Good. Now bring that phat ass over here, drop that robe, and bend over this couch. I'll show you just how much I got my shit together." I was tired as hell, but I had to get up in Trixy before I took a nap.

"Nigga, don't start nothing you can't finish," she stated while pulling me close to her by my shirt collar.

"I knew you wanted some more of this dick."

"Yeah, so what about it? Drop those boxers since you popping off at the mouth so much, and you better not disappoint me," Trixy ordered, pushing me down on the couch in the living room. I couldn't get my jeans off fast enough.

Free pussy was a luxury to me at this point. Trixy had on a wife beater and some booty shorts underneath her robe. She dropped her robe and moved her shorts over to the side, revealing her clean, shaven, wet pussy.

"Damn, baby, you got one of the phattest pussies I've ever seen."

I damn near ripped that wife beater off her and started sucking on her titties as I quickly slid on a condom. As soon as that shit was on, Trixy slid down on my dick and fell right into motion. You would think Trixy was a stripper the way she slid up and down my pole. Everything about Trixy was right. The bitch had a bad body! She had some perfect D cups that were not too firm, not too jiggly. I was mesmerized at the way them shits were bouncing as she rode my dick. Even her nipples were pretty. My tongue was able to get a hold of her nipple and I sucked it like a baby. I grabbed a handful of titties and took turns fitting them right in my mouth.

"Suck these titties, baby," she squealed as she gyrated her hips on my pole. I slid my hands down her sides, squeezed her ass, and gave her a swift spanking. "Ooh, yeah, daddy!" she screamed, and I could feel her pussy getting wetter. This girl was a real freak! I lifted her off of me and threw her on the couch. I was gonna eat the shit outta that pussy. It'd been a long time since I had some of that sweet juice only a woman can make, and a nigga was thirsty right about now. I dove into that pool and went straight to work. I nibbled on her lips and massaged her clit with my tongue. Then I slid two of my fingers deep into her until I found that gushy little button known as the "G" spot. Trixy was buckin' and shaking, trying to squirm away from me as soon as I touched it.

"Oh shit, oh shit! Breezy . . . baby! Oh shit, stop! I'ma come, baby, don't stop! Stop! Oh shit," she screamed as my fingers got soaked with her cum dripping down them. I don't think I ever heard a girl get that confused from busting a nut. I turned her over and started pounding her from behind. Her lips were swollen from her orgasm so she felt even tighter than the last time I hit it. That shit felt like I was getting head at the same time I was stroking it. Damn, this girl had some good-ass pussy. The harder I went in, the more I could feel my nut coming on. I pulled out just as I was about to cum and busted all over her ass. We both flopped on the couch sweaty, sticky, and exhausted. I can't lie, sex with Trixy always wore a nigga out.

***

"Damn!" I got up and looked at the time. It was eight p.m. I'd been sleeping for two hours.

I went to the bathroom, pissed, brushed my teeth, washed my face, then headed to the living room where Trixy was on the computer, checking her Facebook account.

"What up, babe!" I greeted her

"Oh, you finally rose from the dead," Trixy joked.

"I'm saying, you got that knockout pussy, ma. I'll give it to you, you the champ." I laughed.

Not wanting to interrupt Trixy any further, I decided to watch a little TV. I picked up the remote and started flipping though channels. It didn't take long for me to realize something wasn't right.

"Babes, you ain't got no HBO, Cinemax, Showtime, none of that stuff?"

"Nope. I can't afford it. All I have is basic cable. Feel free to upgrade if you like," Trixy said, full of attitude.

With nothing to watch on TV, I figured, fuck it, I'd just grab a beer and watch some old-school DVDs.

"Babes, you got some Heineken in the fridge?" I asked as I headed toward the kitchen.

"I don't think so. But you can go look."

I opened the fridge to see no beer, not even a bottle of water or a pitcher of Kool-Aid. Her shit was empty.

"Babes, you need some groceries. You ain't got shit in here," I announced.

"Yeah, that's what I'm saying. You plan on staying here so plan on fixing that problem. As you can see, I need a sponsor."

As Trixy was talking, shit was marinating. I couldn't even get mad at her. *The shit she is saying is true,* I thought. *The fucked up thing is I can't do nothing to help her. My next paycheck isn't coming in until two weeks from now. I've always been that nigga who get shit done. I was a go-getter. This broke shit ain't even me. I can't be this nigga. I can't even afford to pay a hundred-dollar light bill!* The more I thought, the more I began stressing. I rubbed the cross on my necklace as I thought about my next move. I wondered when God was gonna hold up His end of the bargain and help me deal with all this stuff that was happening. Everything began to replay in my head: the vow I'd taken, Maria and my kids, Ma and her bills and now this situation with Trixy. It was as though the walls were coming in on me. I had to get out of the house.

"I'll be back in a few, shorty," I yelled at Trixy on my way out.

I hit the block heading toward Park Place. I knew I would run into some cats at the barber shop. Ten minutes later I was there, and, just like I figured, Mannie was up there rolling dice.

"Breezy Breeze!" he announced as I walked up.

"What up, Breeze? We ain't seen you since you been out. What, you don't fuck with us no more?" Cats started dapping me left and right.

"Nah, man. It ain't like that. I just had to lay low for a minute before I come out fucking with y'all crazy niggas. You know y'all some trouble-makers. Y'all will have a nigga back in prison," I joked around.

"Yeah, nigga, you ain't lying, 'cause the block is hot."

It felt good to be on the streets again, and it felt even better to know I still had my respect on the streets. I sat and watched as my niggas rolled dice. With one roll, Mannie had won $500. I wasn't even making that from a week's worth of work. Minutes later, I saw this little young dude who used to run for me roll past in a big-body Benz.

"Is that Li'l D who just passed by?" I asked Mannie, to confirm my thoughts.

"Yeah, that's little homie."

"What's that he riding on, twenty-twos?" I asked while checking out his rims. They reminded me of some I had on my Lexus GS before I got locked up.

"Nah, twenty-fours. Those rims set him back at least ten grand."

"Oh, that's how he doing it?" I asked, thinking back to how, before I got locked up, Li'l D was fifteen and running around begging niggas for a few dollars or some work. He was willing to do anything to make a few bucks. Now this little dude was driving a Benz on twenty-four-inch rims.

"Yeah. That nigga doing good now. He Mr. Biggs's right-hand man," Mannie explained.

I had only spent an hour on the block and I'd seen Mannie collect over five grand. These cats were getting it in. These were the same dudes who used to ask me for an eight ball, and now they flying birds. Although I hate to say it, being around all this again really made a nigga feel at home. I felt my hands start to itch from thinking about how things were five years ago. I had the night off, so I decided to go home before I made any fast descisions. I had to get my shit out from Mom's house anyway.

On my walk home, I kept thinking about everything I had accomplished since I dropped out of school. I went from having nothing to being on top of the game. I had the best cars, a beautiful house, a happy wife with my princess and my li'l man standing proud by my side. I was taking care of moms and grandma. Life was good. Most important though, I was respected by all the cats in the streets. Everybody knew who Breezy was and they knew you couldn't fuck with me. I had an army of loyal soldiers and money ran through me like water through my hands. My shit was on point.

When I came home, my moms was passed out on the couch with a cigarette hanging from her hand, and Grandma was already fast asleep in her bedroom. I took the cigarette from her and put it out in the ashtray. I looked down at her. She looked tired and worn out from years of working long hours. *Damn, I can't even help her with a fucking light bill*, I thought as I walked into my room. I started to grab my stuff to take over to Trixy's. As I looked around, I realized I didn't have much to take but three pairs of jeans, some T-shirts, and a pair of sneakers. I couldn't believe what had become of my life.

I went back to thinking about all the things I had lost, then, seeing all that I could gain, I said, "Fuck it." I popped off the necklace Moses had given me and put it in my pocket. Right then I knew this was me. There was no way I could escape the streets. My mind was made up. I was going back in.

"God forgive me for what I'm about to do." I said a silent prayer, then threw my pile of clothes, along with the rest of my shit, in the garbage near the back door. Then I began my walk and headed back toward Park Place. I saw Mannie still rolling dice and I signaled for him. "Yo, Mannie, let me holla at you for a minute."

"What up, B? You look tight. Everything all right?" Mannie said, noticing the change in my demeanor.

"I'm good, man. I was thinking about taking you up on your offer," I said.

"You sure? 'Cause two weeks ago, nigga, you said you wasn't trying to do nothing." Mannie questioned my intentions.

"I know what I said. A couple of weeks ago shit was different."

"Say no more, my nigga. Hop in the car. We can take care of this right now," Mannie said, full of excitement.

Although a nigga would like to believe Mannie was genuinely excited to help me out because he was trying to look out for me, I knew that ain't how it was at all. One, that nigga knew I could push some weight with no problem. He saw me build my empire from nothing. Next, it made that nigga feel good to be able to say that he put Breeze back on. Before I got locked up, nothing moved through the seven cities unless it went through me first. So when I got put away, it gave a lot of other niggas like Mannie a chance to move up. The sad thing was, after all these years, that nigga was still in the same place. Instead of stepping up and filling my shoes, these niggas let some old head nigga, Mr. Biggs, come in and run shit. I couldn't understand how the fuck they let that happen.

"We here. Follow me." I followed Mannie into a decent little crib out by the Lafayette area in Norfolk.

We walked in, and Mannie tried to kick me a whole fucking brick. "Hold on, slow it down, my nig. I ain't trying to rush it. Let me start with a little something and work my way up." I let Mannie know what was up.

"Breeze, what you planning to do? You gon' break this shit down and stand up on the block and compete with all those little nickel and dimebag niggas? That's not even what you do. I know you know people and you can move shit, and we can make a whole lot of fucking paper. I suggest you move around and holla at your people, and let them know you're holding again," Mannie said as he packaged up the cocaine.

I still ended up leaving with a brick, but I couldn't figure out why this nigga would throw me a whole key. It wasn't until I reached Trixy's crib that I figured it out. Mannie had the connect for the coke, but he couldn't move the weight. So this nigga was trying to use me to move it, but he would make almost all the profit money. I wasn't about to do that. I had better plans. Why sell the whole key and make pennies when I could break it down and take it across town? Shit was finally about to change.

As soon as I got settled I planned to call up my nigga Borne. I had met him in prison while he was doing a four-year bid on a crack cocaine distribution charge. On the real, me and that nigga became close after he saved my ass from getting jumped by two big niggas. When I say that nigga saved my ass, I mean that nigga literally saved my ass. I felt like I owed that dude my life. From that day forth, Borne was the only cat I trusted in the pen. He used to always brag about how he had the streets locked before he came in. Unlike me, that nigga was on a mission to lock the streets again as soon as he hit the bricks. He had gotten released six months before me and I hadn't spoken to him since then.

The funny thing is that, when we were locked up, me and Moses used to always talk about making life changes and never going back to the things we did before we got locked up. While I was swearing to change, Borne always vowed he was going back to the streets. He even told me I was talking jail talk and there was no way I was gonna live the straight and narrow. Guess that nigga was right. Borne's only complaint about coming back to the streets was that he'd lost his connect when he got locked up. He knew he would have a problem finding a new connect. Now I was about to be that nigga.

"Borne! What up, nigga?" I yelled into the phone as soon as he picked up.

"Who dis?" he replied, not yet recognizing my voice.

"Your motherfucking lifesaver, nigga," I said, knowing that what I was about to tell him would be music to his ears.

"Oh shit! Breezy Breeze hit the goddamn bricks! How long you been out, nigga?" Borne asked, excited to hear my voice.

"About two weeks."

"Two weeks! And you just hitting a nigga up?"

"Yeah, man. I had to straighten some shit out. You know what I mean. Matter of fact, that's what I'm calling you about right now." I was ready to talk business. "What you been doing out here in the world," I spoke in code to ask Borne if he was hustling.

"Shit, nigga. I'm doing a little something, but not like how it could be. I can't get it how I want it, and when it do come through, cats trying to bust a nigga head open with these prices. I got whole lot of clientele, but not enough merchandise."

"Like I said, nigga, I'm your lifesaver. I got you. I'll hit you tomorrow so we can meet," I said before hanging up the phone. I must say, that night I went to bed with ease. Within minutes I was off to sleep. I had an eight a.m. appointment with my P.O. and I didn't want to be late.

My visit with my P.O. was gravy, like always. Piss clean and still on the job. Mr. Hicks had no complaints with me. Now that that was out the way, it was time for business. I called up Borne.

"Borne! Give the GPS. I'm trying to come see you," I shouted.

"Damn, nigga, I'm on the move right now. How about I come see you in an hour. Cool?" Borne suggested. You remember where you brought the money to my moms when I was locked up?" Borne suggested.

"Yeah, yeah. You remember where you brought that letter to my moms after you got out?" I asked.

"Uh-huh," Borne replied.

"All right, well, come to the green house next door. That's where I'm at." Being that moving around without a whip was hard for me, I was glad he had offered to come to me. It was a relief because I was gonna have to throw on a back-pack, jump on the HRT, and make three fucking transfers just to get to the other side of town where that nigga be at. I wasn't really feeling doing all that, but I knew a nigga gotta do what a nigga gotta do. I made my way back to Trixy's crib to wait for Borne. After an hour and a half that nigga still wasn't there, and I ended up fall-ing asleep.

I awoke to the sound of a horn. I looked out the window to see Borne at the gate. I jumped up and headed out the door. "Goddamn, nigga, you was supposed to be here two hours ago."

"That's how you greet a nigga? You ain't seen me in half a year! I shoulda let them two big niggas kick your ass in the showers when we were in the pen! Then maybe you wouldn't be acting so hard." Borne laughed.

I wanted to laugh with him, but thinking back to that day was much too painful. I couldn't see any humor in that shit at all. I came off the porch and gave my homie some dapps.

"I ain't need your help. I was handling things. Nigga, I had that," I lied, knowing I was losing the fight. I gave my best macho talk in an attempt to cover the terror I felt when reminiscing about that day.

"Yeah, you had your head up against the wall, nigga," Borne said forcing me to face reality.

I needed to change the subject fast, so I quickly turned toward business. "Well, now it's my turn to have your back. Come in the crib so I can holla at you." I opened the door, allowing Borne to walk through.

Trixy and Junior had gone to Ocean Breeze Waterpark for the day, so I didn't have to worry

about any interruptions. I told Borne I could
supply him with the drugs as long as he could
move them. Borne assured me that was not
gonna be a problem. I gave him the package and
he was on his way. To my surprise, two days later
he was ready to re-up. I knew then, business was
gonna go very well.

Chapter 5

Watchful Eye
Mr. Biggs

"Yo, Biggs," I heard a voice say as soon as I picked up the phone. It was the best little soldier I had, Li'l D.

I'd practically raised that boy. When I ran into him he was an eager little cat full of heart and ambition. The thing was, nobody would give him a chance. He kind of reminded me of myself when I was younger. While my brothers were running the streets and deep into the drug game, I was always the schoolboy. I was attending college, working toward my law degree. Every day my brothers would come pick me up from school, and I would ride around with them as they handled their business. I wanted more than anything to be just like them, but they always refused. "These streets ain't for you, boy.

Everybody ain't cut out for this type of shit," my brother would say to me crushing my hopes. So when I ran into Li'l D and saw how much heart that little guy had, I was sure to take him under my wing. Yeah, like any dude new to the game, Li'l D had his flaws, but I saw something in that boy that outweighed any flaw he had, something vital to the game. I saw loyalty and discipline. I knew if I took my time with that boy I could mold him into something great, and that's exactly what I did. Li'l D started off under all the other guys I had on my team.

All those other cats, like Mannie, had been in the game for years. That was their downfall. They felt like they had been in the game so long that no one could teach them anything about it. Not even an old cat like me, who had been hustling since the seventies. I had over thirty years beneath my belt and had never served a day in prison or even been served a warrant. It was by chance I ended up in the game, but it was my approach when dealing with the drug game that got me so far. Being a schoolboy worked to my advantage because I was a thinker. I calculated my every move. I analyzed consequences to each action I would take before I did anything. I figured out long before I entered the drug game that it was carelessness, greed, or envy that caused a man to get either locked up or killed. In fact, it was a combination of all three of those things that ultimately got my oldest brother killed and my other brother sent to prison, leaving me the head of this here empire. When there was no one else left to keep things in motion, I finally had my chance to show everybody I could hold things down. Not only did I hold shit down, but I done it in a much better way and I was still alive to brag about it.

You would think my story about my coming up should have told those young bucks something, but they didn't want to hear it. On the other hand, Li'l D did. I slowly taught him the ropes. He held on to every word I preached, and eventually made something of himself.

"What's up, little homie?" I asked, always happy to hear from him.

"Just checking in to let you know the latest on the streets. I was driving through the hood the other day, and you will never guess who I saw on the block."

"For some reason I think I know exactly who you saw," I said, having a pretty good idea, then continued, "The one and only Breeze."

"Yeah, man. I'd seen him posted up by the barber shop, and when I came back through a few hours later I heard he'd copped a brick from Mannie. Look like he just doing some small work, but you might want to holla at Mannie and see what's really good. I'm surprised that nigga ain't call you and tell you."

"Nah, I ain't heard shit from Mannie. Thanks for the report, D. I'm gonna give Mannie a call." I said before hanging up the phone.

I never really knew what to think of Mannie. At times he would lead me to believe that he was down for the team, and at other times he would move alone like Rambo. I couldn't figure out why Mannie wouldn't call and tell me Breeze was scoring from him.

"Talk to me," Mannie answered right away.

"Nah, that's what I need you to do. Talk to me," I responded.

"What's good, boss?"

"I hear you doing a little business with Breeze?" I said, getting right to the point.

"Oh, yeah, yeah! He came through the hood and hollered at me. Biggs, you know he got a lot of connects. So, I was thinking, if we get that nigga to start buying from us and pushing weight like he did before he got locked up, that shit

could really put money in our pockets. You feel
me?" Mannie explained.

"Money in our pockets or your pockets?" I said
to see where Mannie's head was at.

"Come on, Biggs. Money in my pocket is money in your pockets."

"Okay. So what Breeze talking about?"

"He talking like he ain't really trying to push
no weight, like he wanna just break shit down.
But I know that shit ain't gonna work for him.
Just give him time to try it out and realize that
corner shit is not him. He'll be back for the
weight. Trust me," Mannie said, full of confi-
dence.

"All right, Mannie. Let me know if anything
changes." I hung up the phone, then directed my
attention toward Maria, who had just entered
the room. "Hello, gorgeous," I said to her. I'd
been waiting for her arrival so that I could talk to
her about something.

"Hey, baby." Maria greeted me with a kiss.

"Is there something you want to tell me?" I
asked Maria, always giving her the opportunity
to make things right.

"Biggs, we're not doing this again. What is it?"
Maria said with little tolerance.

"You wanna tell me where Jaden got Jordans from?"

"His father."

"Yeah, I know. He was very proud of his gift from his father. The kids bragged to me about the time they spent at Mount Trashmore with their other daddy. Can you explain to me why I heard that from the children instead of you?" I questioned.

"Honey, I thought it was insignificant," Maria said, reminding me of how our last conversation about Breeze went.

"Why is it you seem to think anything that has to do with your husband is insignificant?"

"Soon-to-be ex-husband and I don't need to be reminded of that. And in response to your question, it doesn't cross my mind because it *is* insignificant. *He* is insignificant," she said with a high-and-mighty attitude.

"Maria, listen, I've said this once and I'm gonna say it again. But just know this is the last time I'm gonna say this. Nothing should go on between you and Breeze without me knowing about it." I reiterated what I'd said in our last conversation that involved Breeze.

"Okay, honey. I got it. I won't make that mistake again," Maria quickly submitted.

"All right, honey. Now, remember what I said. I love you and I give you everything you ask for. All I ask is that you love, honor, and, above all, respect me. As long as it stays that way, we're as good as golden, baby," I said as I hugged my future wife and leaned in for a kiss.

Chapter 6

I Need a Man in My Life
Tanisha

Overdraft fees, voice mail messages, and customer complaints were piled high on my desk. Although I knew it was wishful thinking, I'd really hoped to get everything done by the end of the day. I hated putting things off to the next day when I could do it the same day. My problem was that I had so much to do, I just didn't know where to start. I'd been rushing so much this morning to get the branch up and running that I'd forgotten to stop at Starbucks and grab a cup of my favorite, a white chocolate mocha Frappuccino with a splash of caramel. Now that lunch time was nearing, I felt lost with no energy. I heard a knock at the door as I looked at the piles of paperwork on my desk and contemplated which task to begin with.

"Yes," I answered without looking up.

"Good morning," a deep voice greeted me. I looked up to see it was the gentleman I'd chatted with the other day.

"Hi." I smiled, noticing he looked a lot different since he wasn't dressed in work clothes.

He was dressed in a pin-striped black button-down shirt that had embroidered wings on the back, with dark jeans to match, and black Air Force Ones. I was truly feeling his look. The clean-shaven face and muscular build helped as well. I could smell an old classic of Cool Water cologne lingering in the air as he came near.

"Are you busy?"

"Um, a little. How can I help you?" I inquired, twirling my pearl necklace in my hand and slightly giving him a flirtatious eye.

"I would like to open checking and savings accounts. But before I do that, I want to give you my number again just in case you lost it. I grew up with a lot of women, and I know you have so much stuff in your purse. You're bound to lose something as important as my phone number," he explained. I found his statement rather cute.

"Well, Breeze, I haven't lost your number. And as far as your account, I'm the manager here so I don't usually handle that, but I will be more than happy to get someone to assist you," I explained while paging Madelyn to my office. She was my right-hand person, and I depended on her a lot for the efficiency of the branch.

"You buzzed me," Madelyn stated after walking into the office.

"Yes, I did. Thanks for coming so soon. Madelyn, this gentleman would like to open up a new account."

"Welcome, let's go get started. I just need you to follow to me to my desk," she responded before walking over to her office.

"Thank you for making the decision to open up an account with us. You won't regret it," I assured Breeze.

"I know, but what I don't know is if you would be willing to have lunch with me when I'm finished with the paperwork. Does Jason's Deli sound good? I noticed you had a bag from there the last time I saw you leaving the bank."

"So you've been watching me?" I said, impressed by his observation.

"How could I not? I'm sure you know you're a beautiful woman," He said as he smiled at me.

"Yes, let's do lunch," I agreed, unable to deny such a charming man.

Almost thirty minutes later, Breeze came back into my office.

"Ready for some food?" He smiled.

"Sure am." I grabbed my things and we headed out the door.

Once we arrived at Jason's Deli, Breeze and I hit it off.

"So, Mr. Breeze, tell me something about yourself," I expressed after sipping on fresh-brewed iced tea.

"My story ain't nothing special. My mom and grandmother basically raised me. For years, my mother let me believe that my father was a type of war hero who died for his country. When I turned sixteen, she sat me down and told me the truth," he explained.

"What was the truth?" I inquired.

"He skipped out on her when she was five months pregnant. My mom hasn't seen or heard from him since."

"Wow. How did it make you feel not having a father around?" I asked. I couldn't imagine being without my dad. I grew up with both my parents and, I must admit, I was a daddy's girl all the way.

"Most of the boys in my neighborhood didn't have a father. Sad to say, but it was the norm in my neighborhood. Still is, matter of fact. That's life, I guess. As I got older, I started to hustle on the streets and became really good at it, until I got arrested and sentenced to five years. I just came home from my bid."

"Did you go to jail for drugs?"

"Yeah, but I'm done with that part of my life now. I'm on to better things. You feel me?" Breeze vowed.

"That's good to hear. Do you have any children?" I asked.

"Matter of fact, I do. I have twins, a boy and a girl named Jaden and Kaylyn. They are seven years old. I love those kids so much. Their mother, Maria, puts me on a very limited schedule to see them. A while after I got locked up, she sold my house, and since then, she has my kids looking up to another man to play daddy."

As Breeze spoke a realization hit me. *Maria, Jaden, Kaylyn* . . . this had to be Mr. Biggs's family. I wasn't sure how to ask such a personal question. I approached it with much caution.

"Breeze, do you mind if I ask you a question?"

"You just did, sugar," he replied with a grin.

"Okay, do you mind if ask you something very personal?" I chuckled.

"Nah, we're talking. Go ahead."

"Do you know someone by the name of Mr. Biggs?" I searched his face for some sort of reaction.

"I don't know him but I've heard the name. Why?"

"Well, it's just that the family you described kind of sounds like Mr. Biggs's family. He has seven-year-old twins named Jaden and Kaylyn, and is engaged to a woman named Maria. It's too much of a coincidence that they wouldn't be the people you're speaking about."

"Nah, I assure you that's my family. Maria ran to him when I was locked up," Breeze said with little emotion.

"You know, it's a small world. Mr. Biggs, Maria, and the kids come in the bank every week. Let me tell you, that wife of yours is a handful," I expressed in the most politically correct way I could.

"You don't have to say no more; I was married to the woman. I know all about her. It's either her way or the highway. When Maria was pregnant with Jaden, my mother bought us a crib from Big Lots. It wasn't good enough for her, and she threw it away and had the nerve to let my mother know how she felt. Of course, my mother was hurt behind that. Being with Maria, I had to put up with a lot of shit from her and from her family. At times, I wanted to leave, but I was in that phase where I wanted to stay for the kids. Besides all that though, she was good to me. She loved me and she always made sure I was taken care of. She would make sure I ate, kept up with my gear, and spoiled me with gifts. She stuck by the whole time I was on trial and she visited me regularly. Then a little while after I got locked up, she disappeared along with my kids. In a prison cell, you have a lot of time to reflect on things, you know? I thought I knew Maria. Never once did I think she would take my kids away from me. Then I noticed that all the things she did for me was with my money, so really I was taking care of myself that entire time. All the stuff she got for me was with my own money. Now I wonder if she ever loved me at all," Breeze explained, shrugging his shoulders. For the first time I was able to see a little disappointment in him.

"So how are things with you and Maria now?"

"Not so good. I've only seen my kids once since I've gotten home. She won't even let me talk to them. She's on some bullshit."

"Man, you should be able to have a relation-ship with your kids, though," I added while shaking my head. "Hmm, I can't stand it when the mother doesn't let the father see his kids. There are so many deadbeat dads out there, she should be happy to have a man who actually wants to take care of his children. Why won't she allow you to see your children? Did you do something to her?" I probed in an attempt to understand the situation better.

"No. I've always been a good husband and father. With the exception of me getting locked up, I honestly don't know what her issue with me is," he replied.

"Well, sounds to me like she's just trying to be spiteful. It's just not right." I sighed, feeling sorry for Breeze.

"Deep down, my kids know that I love them. But enough about me, tell me a little about you, Ms. Tanisha," Breeze said, quickly changing the subject. "So, do you have any little ones running around?" he inquired.

"No. I put college and my career first. I figured marriage and kids would come later. To be honest, I've only ever been in one serious relationship."

"Oh, okay. So I got a good girl on my hands. I'll take that."

"Yes, I am." I giggled.

"Tell me about where you came from."

"I grew up in Augusta, Georgia. My God-fearing parents have been married for thirty-one years. I am the epitome of the good-girl image. I was in church every Sunday, received all As, attended Hampton University, and have my MBA. Since eighteen, I've been working for banks off and on, so I decided to stay in the profession. I love numbers. Most of all, I love money," I giggled.

For the next hour we talked, laughed, and joked. It was like we were old friends. It was amazing how we grew up totally different, yet we had so much in common. We both loved old-school comedy, ate dark meat only, and hated Maria's attitude. The time went by so fast. Before leaving, I made sure I gave Breeze my number. Then I sent him a text a few hours later after I got back to the bank. I really enjoyed lunch, and I was definitely looking forward to seeing him again.

Chapter 7

Pockets Getting Fatter
Breeze

"Make it clap!" Trixy insisted, shaking her ass in front of me while I was trying to watch an episode of *Martin* on DVD. That dude was hilarious.

I had to admit, though, her ass was becoming more and more phat courtesy of the multitude of backshots from me. She was making me want to give her another demonstration. After no reaction from me, a disappointed Trixy went into the kitchen to wash the dishes. This girl was very particular how she wanted her house to be. If I let a crumb hit the carpet, it would soon become a heated war with the living room being the battlefield.

As Trixy finished drying the last fork, I came up behind her. I quickly dropped her shorts to the floor. Then I ripped her G-string off of her. I spun her around, lifted her body, and placed her on the counter in one motion. She didn't hesitate to open her legs. I threw my face between her thighs and sucked Trixy's clit while massaging her nipples.

"Damn it, Breeze, I love it when you take this pussy," she whispered while clenching the ends of the refrigerator. Within minutes, she came. Her pussy was so wet that it soaked her inner thighs. My dick was hard and ready to enter. Trixy knew what position I preferred, so without hesitation she turned around to face the refrigerator. I eased my way into her pussy.

"Harder, fuck me, harder," she chanted over and over again. I granted her request. We both came at the same time. Lucky for us we finished right on time, because minutes after we finished, her son came running through the front door.

"Hey, Ma. Hey, Breeze," Junior said while running straight toward the refrigerator.

"What you need out of here?" I playfully jumped in front of the fridge.

"I want some Kool-Aid!" he shouted.

"First tell me something you learned in school today," I demanded.

"Man," he whined. I didn't know what the problem was, but for some reason this little nigga hated school.

"No Kool-Aid until you tell me."

"Mommy?" he begged Trixy for help.

"What did you learn, Junior?" she asked.

"I can't remember."

"Oh, well, too bad. No Kool-Aid for you." I treated Junior like he was my own son.

"Okay, okay. I wrote numbers today."

"All right." I walked over to Trixy's desk and grabbed a piece of paper and a pencil. "Write your numbers, and when you're done your mom will give you some Kool-Aid." I placed the paper and pencil on the kitchen table. Junior sat down and went straight to work. From the corner of my eye I caught a glimpse of Trixy smiling.

Now that I had released a little pent-up frustration and dealt with Junior, it was time to go take care of business. I called up Borne and headed out to go check on him. Instead of meeting him at our usual spot, I met him on the block. It was the first of the month and shit was really rolling, so he wasn't trying to leave and miss out on all that money. I pulled up to the corner store where Borne was standing, and got out of the car. The block was busy as hell. As soon as I saw it, I understood why that nigga ain't wanna leave.

"What up, Borne?" I dapped him up. "I see it's busy as a motherfucker out here."

"It's a'ight," Borne said, downplaying the whole scene.

"A'ight? Niggas lined up like you giving out free government cheese," I said observing what was really going on.

"Yeah, it's popping, but it's hot as a motherfucker out here. Cops been circling every hour. And we got beef with niggas trying to move in on our territory. But fuck all that. Let me get you your paper so you can be on your way," Borne said before pulling out his cell phone and calling his girl up to bring him the money.

I hadn't been waiting two whole minutes before I was on the ground with my goddamn face in the dirt. One minute, I was leaning against the wall, had just popped open a cold Heineken, and was about to take a sip. Next thing I knew, I heard a car screeching and people start screaming. Before I could throw myself to the floor, I heard two shots, then bullets ricochet off the wall right next to me.

What the fuck! was all that ran through my mind. Shit was happening so fast. I was pissed that I ain't have shit on me, so I couldn't do shit but lie down until it was over. From my angle, I saw Borne pull out a .45 Desert Eagle and start shooting back in the opposite direction. That's when shit really got crazy. Bullets started coming from everywhere. Although it only lasted about two minutes, that shit seemed like an hour. That shit had me feeling like I was in Desert Storm.

"Fuck, they got little homie," I heard a dude yell once the firing stopped. His statement was followed by a woman's cry, a girl's frantic scream, and niggas' shouts of retaliation. When I got a little closer, I could see dude had caught one in the neck and was bleeding uncontrollably. Needless to say, that nigga died before the ambulance arrived.

Damn, this is crazy. I gotta get the fuck outta here, I thought as I watched and took in all that was going on around me.

"Yo, let's blow this joint," Borne said. It was exactly what I wanted to hear. We hopped in my car and went to his girl's crib. I grabbed my loot and was out.

"What a hell of a night," I said to no one in particular as I drove off.

The next morning, I went to see my parole officer. The more I showed up for appointments and my piss test was in good standing, the more he began to loosen up. Plus, my P.O. mentioned that O.G. had put in a good word for me. As I was on my way to pick up my check, I started thinking about how different my life would be a year from now. I knew I was about to be on the come up and nobody was going to stop me.

"Morning," I greeted the O.G. as I walked in.

"Good morning to you too," he responded before looking me up and down. "So, son, how you doing?" he inquired.

"A'ight." I nodded.

"Here's your check," he stated, handing it to me.

"Thanks, and I appreciate you putting in a good word for me with my P.O."

"No problem. Boy, you're at a crossroads. Now, don't make me tell that parole officer of yours that you're fucking up."

"I ain't been late or not showed up for work one time, O.G. man, what are you talking about?" I questioned, getting a little pissed off. O.G. was always in my ass for something and I was getting tired of it.

"What? You think I haven't noticed the new clothes on your back and the jewelry on your wrist and neck? You can't buy none of that shit on what you make, son."

"Okay, I picked up a few things. So what!" I barked.

"Listen, I couldn't care less if your ass is mad at me. You hustling again! Don't try to insult my intelligence or cut me off. I got the motherfucking floor right now! You need to take the right path. Otherwise, you will end up back in jail or in a coffin. I've been down that path, so I'm just trying to warn you. You have been given a second chance and you have the potential to do something great. Don't fuck it up. Get the fuck off the corner, son!"

I didn't want to disrespect the O.G., but I had to wonder what the fuck I could possibly do so great by pushing a fucking mop. "I'll see you at six," I replied and walked off, heading to the car. The O.G. was tripping, and since a nigga couldn't smoke, I needed to get a drink.

After I stopped at Marvin's, a local bar where no one dares to bother you, I decided to give Tanisha a call. I knew hearing her voice would get me out of the slump I was feeling.

"Hey, you," she said as soon as she picked up.

"What's going on?"

"Oh, nothing much. Just sitting here at work. I forgot I have to close tonight because I gave two of my customer representatives the afternoon off," she explained.

"Aren't you a nice manager," I added.

"I know," she laughed.

"Well, I was trying to see if you could meet me for dinner tonight. You pick the place," I offered.

"What about the Cheesecake Factory around eight o'clock?"

"Yeah, that's good for me. I'll see you then. Enjoy the rest of your day," I replied.

"You as well," she responded before hanging up the phone.

As soon as I hung up with Tanisha, I called Maria.

"What is it, Breeze?" she answered after I called ten times back to back.

"You know exactly what it is, Maria. I want to see my kids."

"I don't know who the hell you think you're talking to. Don't mistake me for one of your little ghetto chicks."

"I'm not even trying to argue with you. I just want to see my kids." I pleaded.

"Breeze, I can't stand the thought of you let alone the sight of you. The only reason I am willing to allow you to see the children is because they keep asking about you. I can't understand why or how they even like you in the first place. You're lucky my facial was rescheduled so I have a little bit of free time today. I'm picking the kids up from school at three. We can meet you at Jillian's at three thirty." Maria dictated what time and where I could see the children.

Not wanting to put up a fight, I readily agreed and hung up the phone. At least something positive was going to come out of this afternoon. Maria had agreed to let me see the kids again.

I quickly got myself together and headed downtown toward Waterside. I spotted Maria and the kids as soon as I walked through the door. A few days ago, she saw me in the MacArthur mall and she acted as if she didn't even know me. As I walked up to her at Jillian's, I could tell she was checking me out.

"You're on time. That's a good thing," she commended me.

Once again, the kids were reluctant to give me hugs and kisses. I didn't get mad, because I knew it would take time for them to get accustomed to me being in their lives permanently. They were so young when I went away.

"Of course I'm on time. I know it's still a pet peeve of yours. I bought you a little something," I explained, handing her a dozen roses.

"Thank you," she replied, trying hard not to crack a smile.

"There are eight deep pink roses to say thank you for allowing me back into our kids' lives, three yellow roses because I care about you, and a single red rose because a part of me will always love you, Maria," I responded. I could tell Maria was touched by my gesture. She even let me have an extra hour with the kids.

Chapter 8

Gotta Get Mine
Trixy

It was time I eased up on Breeze. I could tell he was starting to get tired of my bitching and moaning about dirty dishes and leaving the toilet seat up. The truth was, I really enjoyed having him live with me. I'd never told anyone, but I was devastated when I heard he got locked up. Ever since I let him take my virginity, I'd always felt a special connection with him. I fucked with a few dudes through the years but I never did stop thinking about Breeze. When I heard he was being released, I counted the days for him to get out and come back home. Even though I knew he had his wife and kids, I had made a vow to myself that I'd make him mine eventually. When I saw him the day he got out, I had to hide my excitement when I realized Maria had left his ass. She had made it real easy for me to get him right where I wanted him; in my bed each night.

Now, lately I noticed he had been talking and seeing his kids a little more often than before. The last thing I needed was for her to be slightly nice to Breeze and fuck up his head. Breeze was my man now and I planned on keeping it that way. He was the man in my life as well as the man in my son's life. For the first time, Junior had a man to look up to, and Breeze was so good with him. It put a smile on my face each time Breeze played football or basketball with him, or when they played video games together. It made me even happier when Breeze did homework with Junior. We were Breeze's family now, and I would do anything to keep it that way.

I knew Breeze was trying to go the straight-and-narrow way when he first got home, but I knew the memories of his previous kingpin status would be dancing in his head at night. Breezy Breeze from the streets was back and it was time niggas started to watch out. The king was about to rebuild his empire, and I was certain that I was gonna be the queen sitting on the throne next to him. For the past week, I'd been waiting for him to say anything, and I mean anything, about helping him out. Once he started rising to the top, I wanted to make sure I was the only ride or die chick by his side. A street nigga loved a down-ass bitch, and I was gonna show Breeze I was just that chick. I wasn't just doing it for myself; more importantly, I was doing it for my son. We both needed to make sure Breeze was a permanent part of our lives, but my son needed him more than anything.

"Morning. You up early," Breeze greeted me, yawning.

"So are you," I confirmed, looking at the clock in the kitchen.

"Yeah, I have a few things to take care of." He nodded.

"You hungry?"

"Yeah, I could go for a little bacon, scrambled eggs with cheese—"

"And toast with butter on the side," I stated, cutting him off.

"That's my girl," he confirmed before giving me a kiss on my neck.

"Listen, I need you to do me a small favor. I made a promise to take Junior to the mall to get the new Jordans this morning so I need you to handle something for me. I want you to take this bag to Mannie, and he gonna give you back a small duffle bag. You think you can handle that?"

"Yes," I assured him.

"Good. The bag is in the closet on the left-hand side," he explained after turning on the television in the living room.

Breeze was talking to me like I didn't know what was going on. I knew I was taking Mannie money and he was giving me drugs in return, but it was cool. I had this. This was nothing to me. The only fear I may have had was wondering if a nigga would rob me. But once Breeze said the name Mannie I knew I was good. Mannie was my nigga. We went way back. It started off as a fuck thing but I eventually became his ride or die chick. Eventually things between us ended, but I'd been his little homie every since.

An hour later, I pulled up at a Virginia Beach public library. It was an easy exchange. I could tell Mannie's eyes were more concentrated on my ass than on the money I was bringing him.

"Damn, that ass getting phat," he said as I walked up to his car.

"Whatever, Mannie, I'm working. No time for play," I said jokingly.

"Oh, so you working for Breeze now. You giving him that pussy like you used to give me?" Mannie asked while staring at my camel toe.

"That ain't your business," I snapped.

"It's all good. At least you keeping it in the family," Mannie said as I got out of the car.

I shook my head when I returned to my car. It was sad how a nigga always had sex on his mind. Mannie didn't even count the money. He was too busy making passes at me. I could have robbed his ass if I were a real grimey-type chick. That's one thing I liked about Breeze, he didn't think with his dick. That nigga was about his paper.

When I got back to my place, Breeze was so impressed with the completed task at hand, that he offered for me to be his road dawg. I had passed the test! Of course, I agreed with no delay. After all, that was my plan from day one. Later on that night I celebrated with wild sex. I popped an ecstasy pill and fucked the shit out of Breeze. The X had me going hard that night. It had me going so hard that I was sucking Breeze's dick, giving him the blow job of his life. I was really feeling my head game. Superhead ain't had shit on my moves! I slurped, licked, and sucked my way down to his balls, where I rotated them in and out of my mouth while I stroked his shaft. From the way he was moaning, I could tell Breeze was feeling it, so I decided to get real freaky with it. I stuck my tongue in his ass! That ended up being the biggest mistake of my life. Breeze jumped up and yelled, "Get the fuck off me." Then he pushed me so hard I flew off the bed and into the wall. That shit freaked me out. That nigga reacted like a Vietnam veteran with post-traumatic stress disorder. I didn't know what the fuck that was about, but I made a mental note never to go that route again.

Chapter 9

Stand by My Man
Tanisha

I looked out the window to see Breeze standing outside, blowing on a car's horn. I grabbed my bag and raced out the front door. We were running late for church.

"Oh, you got a new rental?" I asked, noticing that Breeze was driving a different car from the Toyota Camry rental I had seen him driving lately.

"Nah. This is me. You like it?"

"You bought a new car, Breeze?" I asked, surprised.

"Yeah. It's just a little something. I figured for the money that I was spending on rentals I could just buy my own little ride. You feel me?" Breeze tried justifying purchasing a new car.

"Yeah, I guess," I responded.

As we were riding down Virginia Beach Boule-vard in Breeze's new Chrysler 300 with a naviga-tion system, I began to wonder how he was able to purchase such a car. I knew he didn't make that much as a janitor. My worst fear was that he was back to selling drugs. I began to worry that, this time, he may not end up in a prison cell. Instead, his fate could be a coffin. My thoughts began to race. *Should I ask him? I don't want him to get mad at me. Do I really want to get involved with someone who sells drugs? My daddy would be livid with me, and my mother would do more than just yell at me; she'd prob-ably lay hands on me.* I figured for the time being I wouldn't jump to any conclusions. I de-cided to just observe Breeze for any signs of him being back into the drug game. Minutes later we'd arrived at church.

"Saints, there's one more thing left to do," Pastor Gregory announced.

"It's offering time," a woman shouted out as she stood up. "Praise the Lord!"

"Yes, Sister Richards, you are correct, it is in-deed offering time," he assured her.

"Amen," a man shouted in front of us while waving his check in the air.

"God loves a cheerful giver. If you're not giving from the heart, don't bother putting a penny in the basket. You will not get blessed that way," the pastor preached.

I couldn't agree with him more, I thought as I pulled a crisp fifty-dollar bill out of my purse. I may not have had 10 percent to give, but I did have something. Out of the corner of my eye, I saw Breeze pull out a one hundred-dollar bill. I had to admit that I was impressed. I continued to watch him and listened closely as I heard him whisper, "Please forgive me, Lord." I didn't know what Breeze had done, but I was thankful he knew who to go to for forgiveness. That alone eased my heart.

As the ushers assembled around each church row, the choir began singing a song called "A Cheerful Giver." I'd been attending the Assembly Church of God in Norfolk since I moved to the area. These people welcomed me with open arms and I'd been going there ever since. They were more like family to me, and I hoped Breeze wanted to become part of the family as well. We'd been talking and spending a lot of time together over the past few weeks, and I must admit

I was really feeling him. I knew deep down that I was feeling him a lot more than he was feeling me, though. I tried not to show it to Breeze, but I knew I was falling for him. Sometimes I wondered if Breeze was even able to love or trust anymore after what Maria did to him. I was sure Maria had turned his heart cold. This was a first for me. Back home, men fell to their knees for my hand, and it hadn't been any different when I moved to Norfolk. That is, until I met Breeze, and now I found myself on the other end of the spectrum.

"Thank you for inviting me to church," Breeze said as he opened the car door for me.

"You're welcome. I hope you will come back again." I giggled.

"Yeah, I will." He nodded.

"That's good to hear," I replied, taking comfort in his words.

"Where to now, Ms. Tanisha? Are you hungry?"

"Yes, I am."

"Captain George's, here we come," Breeze announced before turning up the radio. I definitely had a taste for seafood. This restaurant had a sixty-item buffet, but we all knew everyone went for the countless plates of crab legs.

Minutes later, we arrived at a busy Captain George's. There was a short wait, but it was well worth it. It didn't take long for someone to show us to our seat, and we wasted no time digging right in.

"I have a little something for you," Breeze mentioned after I finished my first plate.

"What is it?" I asked, excited.

Out of his pocket, he pulled a box. Enclosed was a Tiffany necklace with a key charm. "The key unlocks my heart. Always remember that," he explained.

"Thank you," I replied with a bit of worry in my voice.

"Baby, what's wrong? You don't like it?" Breeze asked, concerned.

"I love it. In fact, you did well, really well. It's just that you and I both know on a cleaning crew salary you can't afford this. I may have grown up on the other side of the tracks, but I do have some street smarts. Breeze, please be honest with me are you back to selling drugs?" I inquired in a low voice.

"I've always been honest with you, Tanisha, so I'm not gonna start lying now. Yes, I am," he confirmed.

"Wow," I replied, disappointed. "How could you take such a risk, Breeze? I mean, you just got home."

"Tanisha, it won't be for long. It's only until I get back on my feet. I'm not even doing much. I hardly even touch it. I just get it from my man, then give it to some other cats across town. I got dreams too, you know. Dreams cost money. You know that." Breeze tried his best to give me good reason for his actions.

"Have you looked for a better paying job?" I asked, trying to suggest a more safer way for him to make that money.

"No, I have not. I'm a felon, Tanisha. Ain't nobody trying to hire me. All they see is a record and they want no part of that. I guess felons aren't worth the trouble. Babe, don't let this spoil things. We're having such a great lunch," he suggested, taking my hand.

"Will you promise to quit soon? I can't be sitting here worrying about you being all wrapped up in the drug game."

"Agreed," Breeze quickly replied. I couldn't tell if he was being honest or just wanted to end the conversation. I could only trust and pray that he was telling me the truth.

***

I began to think that Breeze, his drug game, and his drama may be more than I could chew. I didn't want to be up at all times of the night thinking the worst, but, unfortunately, that's exactly what was going on. I had this fear of being woken up by a phone call in the middle of the night saying he was back in jail. I knew that could get real old, real quick. *I'm not sure I can do this. I deserve better. I deserve more. Why is this happening to me again?* My head started to spin as I thought back to the days I dated Jose. It seemed like history was repeating itself.

Jose was my first love, and he was everything I'd ever dreamed of in a man. He was my Mexican lover, as I used to call him. He stood tall at six feet even, with a rich caramel complexion, and big dark brown puppy eyes. A lot of my friends immediately stereotyped, and warned me about getting involved with a Hispanic man because they were known to be possessive. Jose proved them all wrong, though. He treated me like a queen. He was always loyal, respectful, gentle, and funny. After only a year of dating, Jose proposed to me. It was also at that point that he introduced me to another side of his life. Jose was part of the Mexican cartel. This piece of information was too much for me to take in. At first, I told myself I could roll with it, but when reality set in about the kind of life I would live being married to someone in his position, I knew I couldn't marry him. Being the wife of someone in the Mexican cartel would mean a life of terror. I would have to be on the defense and prepared for anything, because his enemies could come for me at any moment. I was not naive to how the streets got down, and in the streets, no one is ever spared. You can be killed just by association, but family is the first thing they go for. I was smart enough to realize I would not be able to live that kind of lifestyle, and I could not see myself bringing kids into a situation like that. It really hurt Jose when I gave him the ring back, but there were no hard feelings between us. He told me I would always have a piece of his heart, and if I ever needed anything, he would be just a phone call away.

Now I was faced with Breeze being in the drug game. I didn't know what to do. I really liked Breeze and I didn't want to lose him.

I spent hours and hours thinking. That's when it hit me: "I'll introduce Breeze to Jose," I said to no one in particular.

Breeze said selling was a temporary situation to get him back on his feet. From the way he explained things, it would take him months before he started to see any real money. I knew if I hooked him up with Jose he could make his money faster, which meant he would be able to get out of the drug game earlier than anticipated. I wasn't sure if I was making the right decision by introducing them, though. I didn't want him to think that I was encouraging his hustle, but I really wanted him to be in and out. I loved him and I wasn't willing to lose another good man and potential husband. I wasted no time calling Breeze and telling him all about my plan. He was a little reluctant at first, and asked a lot of questions, but by the end of our conversation he was on board.

Chapter 10

No Room For a Side Chick
Trixy

"Suck that dick, I'm about to come," Breeze whispered as he pulled my head closer in between his legs. I wasted no time sliding off the condom and getting down to business. I was sure to stay far from his asshole as I finished him off. The incident that happened that night I had popped the ectasy pill still haunted me. I stayed on point with giving him top-notch blow jobs every time, but I was extra careful not to go anywhere near his back door.

"Ah . . . that's it, Trixy. Fuck," he said as I felt his dick swell and bust out. When he came I swallowed every drop of his cum. It tasted bitter. I guess because of all that Heineken Breeze had drunk.

"You ready for another go-round with Ms. Puss?" I asked after coming up for air.

"Nah, I'm about to hop in the shower and get ready for work," he replied. I was a little disappointed because I was hoping to get a nut too, but I wasn't about to start bitching. At this moment in my life, I couldn't be better. This nigga was paying every bill in this house and giving me money on the side. What meant more to me than the money was that Breeze was being a father to my son. A bitch was happy! The only complaint I had was that Breeze strongly needed to invest in a money counter because my hands were starting to hurt from counting his stacks. A bitch's hands were full of papercuts! Plus, a money counter would cut down on time and human errors. Every now and then, a stack ended up short or over and I would have to do it all over again. Well, when it came up over I would recount it, but when it was short I would just keep it moving. I knew most of the time it was short because I didn't hesitate to take a little extra for myself. And since he'd stopped fucking with Mannie and started dealing with those Mexicans, it had become easier and easier to shave a little off the side. Breeze had more and better product and his clientele had grown, too. He was pushing straight weight, no more cooking up crack and dealing with niggas on the block. Needless to say, money was coming in left and right. At times I felt like Breeze had more money than he could keep up with. That's why when I took a few bucks it went unnoticed.

While Breeze was in the shower, I noticed his phone wouldn't stop ringing. I knew it couldn't be Maria. That bitch hardly ever called. I tiptoed in the bedroom and quickly went through this phone. I couldn't believe a new chick was on the scene. Her name was Tanisha and she had sent him a text saying: I love you and miss you.

"What the fuck?" I said to no one in particular.

I knew Breeze had to have been seeing this chick for a while. Sickness suddenly fell over me. I felt faint and then nauseated. I took a few deep breaths and gathered myself. Then anger kicked in.

"Who the fuck is Tanisha?" I questioned after barging in the bathroom and opening up the shower curtain.

"What?"

"Breeze, you fucking heard me. Who the fuck is Tanisha? Are you fucking her?"

"Be cool, Trixy," he suggested, hopping out of the shower, wrapping a towel around his waist.

"On the first day you came home I was there for you. Breeze, you didn't have shit and I took you in, and this is how you repay me?" I shouted.

"I don't need this," Breeze insisted while grabbing a huge duffle bag and throwing his things into them.

"That's a'ight. Go ahead and leave. Next time you are in a shitty bind, don't come knocking on my door!" I snapped.

"I can't believe you're acting this way."

"One more thing I need you to know," I shouted.

"What's that?" Breeze asked, shaking his head, almost at the front door.

"Junior is . . ." I paused and took a deep breath. "Junior . . ." I paused again. For some reason, I just couldn't get the words out.

"What about Junior, Trixy?" Breeze had a sudden look of worry on his face. "Trixy? What is wrong with Junior?" He dropped his bag and headed back toward me.

To see his reaction about Junior really tugged at my heart, but I still didn't have the courage to tell him, so I just made something up off the top of my head. "Junior is really gonna miss having you around. Get out of my house," I shouted, trying my best to cover my hurt feelings.

Without a fight, Breeze picked up his bag and headed out the door. I couldn't believe he could just up and leave like that after everything I did for him. I ran to the door so I could see him through the blinds. Right then I knew this nigga was just using me all along and never gave a fuck about me; not once did he bother to look back.

Chapter 11

Tricks of the Game
Breeze

Although I was a little hesitant at first, I have to say I was glad Tanisha had put me on with the Mexicans. The whole ex-boyfriend thing was fucking with me, but when that paper started coming in, I forgot all about that shit. It was straight money on my mind. As they say, "Money over bitches." The coke was coming in and I was moving it out just as fast. I knew at the rate I was going I would have the seven cities on lock all over again. This time I would do it better than the first. Only this time, I was gonna be smarter about what to do with my money, so that I could walk away from the game and be free from the street hustle. With Tanisha on my side, there was no way I could fuck up. That girl stayed on me about investments, IRA accounts, CDs, and a whole lot of other intelligent banking bullshit that I didn't understand. One thing I did know was that in the end I was gonna be able to walk away from the game and live life as a legitimate wealthy man.

Since Trixy had gone the hell off on me, I had to find another dedicated soldier to be by my side. I was mad things had gone down the way they did, 'cause she did a lot for me. It's fucked up she had to start catching feelings and ruin what we had. I never told that girl I loved her or that we were even together. She knew from day one we had a certain agreement. She really stepped out of line the way she came at me, questioning me about my personal business like that. Oh, well though. You know how the saying goes: hoes and money don't mix.

The problem now was finding someone I could trust to take her spot. Trixy was my right-hand person and my second set of eyes. She knew all about the business. She was streetwise and trained to shoot without hesitation. She was a ride or die bitch. We had a perfect working relationship and the sex was always good. With the exception of the asshole incident, I couldn't give any complaints about sex with Trixy. Thinking back to that night, I was wrong for pushing her across the room like that. That shit wasn't her fault. I had some real fucked-up issues with all that anal stuff from when I was locked up. Sometimes I wondered if a nigga needed counseling.

The truth was, those two niggas Borne saved me from in the showers that day were about to rape me. Dudes was mad 'cause I had fucked up one of their boys for disrespecting me. I beat that bitch's ass that day, so the next morning, they came after me for some retaliation. And they really wanted to fuck my ass up, literally! Being in there, I got used to all that homo shit going on, but I ain't ever planned on participating in it. After fighting them off for a couple of minutes, I knew it was a battle I wasn't gonna win. Niggas had me in position when Borne walked in and saw what was going on. I couldn't help but wonder what would have happened if Borne wouldn't hadn't stepped in. That was some shit that had been haunting me ever since, and it messed with my head almost on a daily basis. No matter how hard a nigga tried to erase it from his memory, it would always reappear.

Always about my business, I wasted no time putting out word that I was recruiting soldiers. Shit, the economy was bad, but bills still had to get paid, and with niggas losing their jobs left and right, I knew it wouldn't be long before someone stepped up to the plate. I went to Marvin's to ease my head a little bit.

"Another one?" the bartender asked at my favorite spot.

"Naw, I'm good," I replied after sipping on my last Hennessy.

"Sup?" said a dude sitting at the bar two stools down.

"Mannie, what's going on?"

"Breeze, I wanted to ask you the same thing. I haven't seen you in a while," he mentioned.

"Yeah, thanks but no thanks, I don't need you anymore."

"Nigga, I put you back on and now you don't need me anymore?" he replied, inching closer to me.

"Bartender, I'll pay for his drink," I responded, and threw down a hundred-dollar bill.

I wasn't going to get upset over Mannie's little outburst. *Fuck him, I'm looking out for me and mines only*, I thought as I walked away. As I headed to the car, Trixy called me for the fourteenth time. This girl was relentless. I didn't want to answer the phone. I didn't feel like dealing with her right now. Besides, I needed to lie down and catch up on some much needed rest.

I headed toward my new place. I guess you can call it a coincidence or perfect timing, 'cause I had bought it, like, two days before the shit with Trixy went down. It wasn't in my head to move out of Trixy's when I bought it. I had planned on keeping it as a private getaway for when I needed to get away from all the bullshit. My own secret spot in the Hamptons Apartments right near the water. Since Trixy came out her face on some relationship-type drama, I decided to turn it into a nice little bachelor pad.

I made it home and threw myself on my new king-sized bed. I hadn't bought anything else for the house yet but I made sure I had a big, comfortable bed. Besides, I was meeting Tanisha for breakfast in the morning and we had plans to go furniture shopping afterwards. I couldn't wait to see her face. There was something about that girl that had a hold on me. My thoughts about her were interrupted with my phone vibrating with a text from Trixy. I turned it off to avoid having to deal with it 'cause I knew she'd be calling again soon. I refused to let her fuck up my relaxation time.

I woke up early and got myself ready to spend the day with my favorite girl. I picked Tanisha up and we had a nice breakfast at Cracker Barrel. After breakfast, Tanisha and I headed straight to the furniture store.

"Babe, do you like this hazelnut set for the living room?" Tanisha inquired with her eyes glued to a set that was in the middle of the display floor. It came with a couch, love seat, ottoman, and reclining chair. The reclining chair brought back memories from my happier days. Every night, when I came home, Maria and the kids would greet me at the door. After dinner, I always sat in this Simon pushback reclining chair in the movie room. The kids were still small enough to both sit on my lap, so I would recline in the chair with them and we would usually fall fast asleep.

"I like it." I nodded to her and told the salesperson to add it to the list. From her picks so far, it seemed Tanisha was really hooking up my little spot for me. It's true what they say, that a feminine touch goes a mighty long way. She had a knack for designing. I let her pick everything out, from the bedroom to the rug for the front door, and I knew the place was going to look great. Tanisha had so much going for herself. She definitely was the total package. At first glance, and because of her background, you would think she was snooty and stuck-up but she was far from it. She was so smart, beautiful, and down-to-earth. What was most important to me was that she was honest and she stuck by my side, even though she wasn't too crazy about what I was doing. That meant a lot to me, and I truly felt as though I could trust her.

"All right, folks, the grand total is $6,048.90. Will this be cash or charge?" the salesperson inquired.

"Cash," I insisted while placing hundreds and fifties in his hand.

We made arrangements to have the furniture delivered then we headed out.

"So what are the plans for tonight?" Tanisha asked as I pulled into her driveway.

"You, me, a bottle of pinot grigio, and a long hot bath," I suggested.

"Sounds like a plan." She giggled before kissing me on the lips and heading to her front door. Another thing I loved about Tanisha was that she didn't ask a lot of questions.

Now that I had spent a little time with Tanisha, the next stop was my grandma's crib. Although they were right next door when I was living with Trixy, I hadn't seen them since the day I moved out.

"Hmm, I haven't seen you in a while," Ma acknowledged after taking a puff of her cigarette.

"Hello to you too, Ma," I replied, handing her a box of Newports.

"Grandma, he bought gifts. Damn, I was down to my last pack 'til payday next week. Thank you, baby," Ma responded while giving me a hug.

"Open the box," I suggested.

"Oh my Lord," Ma screamed as she opened the box. "Let me sit down on this couch so I can get myself together." She rejoiced while counting $1,000 from the box.

"This is for you," I announced while handing Grandma a box of Whitman's chocolates. Those were her favorite.

"Thanks, honey," she responded.

"One more thing, Grandma, here's two hundred dollars for the building fund at your church. When I was here that's all I would hear you talking about when you were on the phone with your church buddies." I handed her the money.

"Boy, I hope for your sake you're not on those streets again," Grandma stated concerned.

"Grandma, don't worry, I'm not on those streets. Being behind bars isn't a good look for me," I replied, lying through my teeth. I figured if she didn't know the truth, then she wouldn't be up endless nights praying for me.

"Okay," she responded, not sounding too convinced.

"Let me get going. I have to get to work," I informed them.

The truth was that I was on my way to see Maria and the kids at Mount Trashmore, but I didn't dare tell Ma that. That would lead to an hour of her ranting and raving about "that money-hungry, mixed-breed bitch." And I wasn't in the mood to hear that shit.

I was dressed in nothing but labels: Louis Vuitton sneakers and belt, True Religion jeans, and a plain white Polo shirt. To top it off, I added a white gold chain with matching bracelet, and Louis Vuitton shades. I knew these types of things would get Maria's attention. I also made sure I had a little something for her. I was starting to see that the gifts softened her up a bit. I hoped this would get Maria to take her tight leash off the kids. It's sad, but at times I felt as if she treated them more as property than human beings by dangling them in my face. As always, I made sure I arrived early for my meeting with Maria and the children. It wasn't long after I'd gotten there that they came running up to me.

"Hey, Daddy," Kaylyn greeted me from a distance.

"Hey, you," I replied giving the kids hugs. I bought a bag full of Wii games and DS games. I was learning what they preferred, courtesy of Maria.

"Hi." Maria smirked. I saw her trying to check me out on the sneak.

"How are things?" I asked while handing her a wad of money. It was $3,000. She didn't hesitate to count it carefully.

"Thank you." A huge smile came across her face.

I couldn't help but notice the scent of Escada Magnetism perfume. She had worn it for years. Maria was wearing a summer dress that almost hung to the ground. I had to admit, she looked sexy as hell.

After placing the money in her oversized Gucci bag Maria continued, "The kids are fine, but I'm not so great."

"What's going on?" I asked right away.

"Well, Biggs is a good father to the kids—"

I interjected before Maria could even finish her statement. "I'm the only daddy they got!" I said, irritated by what Maria was saying.

"Breeze, are you finished with your tantrum? I'm really not in the mood," she explained while shaking her had.

"I'm sorry, go ahead." I gathered myself a bit.

"As I said, Biggs is a good father to the kids. But it's different with me. He doesn't pay attention to me anymore. I'm just there, like the crown molding on the wall: pretty to look at, but has no real use or purpose. Business has been slow for him, and that's pretty much been his main focus lately," Maria explained.

"I'm here for you anytime you need to talk," I assured her. Deep down I was thrilled as hell to know her relationship with the almighty Mr. Biggs was going downhill.

"Thanks, I appreciate that. I just want you to know that I never tried to take the kids away from you. You left us, and you lied about how much time you were really facing. Breeze, you told me you only had three years. I was angry and just wanted to hurt you for going to prison. I wanted you to feel the pain I was feeling." Maria expressed her feelings for the first time. Now things were finally starting to make sense.

"You have a point. I should have told you the truth," I agreed.

It felt good for Maria and I to finally air things out and patch things up. We talked a little more and agreed to make things work for the sake of the children. After playing with the kids and stuffing them with chips, candy, and soda from the snack machine, they were on their way.

After I left Maria and the kids, I went to see this little homie Borne had put me down with. Since I had stepped my game up, so had Borne. Now instead of him being on the block, he was cooking up and niggas was copping from him, breaking that shit down and hitting the block. Borne had gotten a few trap houses throughout the seven cities. His newest spot was out of Park Place. I knew that was Mannie's territory, but I ain't give a fuck. I was all about my dollars.

I pulled up to Borne's spot on Twenty-sixth Street, hollered at a couple of friends on my way up to the crib, then let myself in.

"Sup," I acknowledged him after entering his house.

"Man, I've been blowing you up all day," the little homie explained.

"I had to handle some things. You have my attention now, nigga. What's going on?" I wondered what was so damn urgent.

"Last night, some niggas I don't know ran up and got me for ten grand."

"Do you know who could have done it?" I asked, even though I had a pretty good idea who it could have been.

"Nah, I told Borne about it and I got my boys seeing if anybody is willing to talk," he replied with a hint of fear in his voice.

"All right, but you know, I'm still going to need that back," I said to the little homie. I couldn't let a nigga think a loss like that was acceptable.

"Without a doubt. I got you, Breeze." He nodded before I headed back out the door.

As I was driving, I was thinking at ten miles per minute. At first, I was thinking that Mannie probably sent some niggas to the crib, but this little nigga's actions was leading me in a different direction. I had to wonder if that nigga was trying to play me. Deep inside, I knew this was the shit I had to look forward to when dealing with new cats. Although it went against everything in me, I knew I had to get Trixy back on the team. Sure I would take a few small losses but never a ten grand loss. I wasted no time heading to her crib. I didn't even call first.

I knocked on the door knowing Trixy could see me through the peephole. She didn't answer at first, but I knew she was home because her car was parked outside. I kept knocking, knowing she probably was looking right at me. I knew she was getting pleasure by making me stand outside and wait

"Breeze, what do you want? I ain't giving out free pussy so go the fuck somewhere else," Trixy yelled through the door, finally acknowledging my presence.

"Trixy, I didn't come here for that. I came to see my little nigga. Let me in." I tried using her son as an excuse, although I honestly did miss Junior.

"Breeze, you know Junior is at school," she spat.

"I know, I know." I stopped playing games and got serious. "On the real, I got a proposition for you, if you're willing to listen." I was sure to keep it strictly business this time.

"I'm listening," she stated while cracking the door open. "Don't even think about coming in."

"The bottom line is I need you back in the game with me," I confessed.

"How much?" she asked.

"How much what?"

"How much you gone pay me?" she clarified. I guess she was about business too.

I gave my first offer. "One grand a week."

"Nah, you got to come harder than that. I want two grand a week. Matter of fact, right now, I could use two hundred dollars to pay my light bill," Trixy spat.

"Okay, so how about fifteen hundred a week, plus I got you on that light bill right now." I gave my final offer.

"You got a deal," Trixy agreed as she opened her door all the way

"All right, you start next week," I agreed while handing her the money for her light bill.

"Cool."

"One more thing. I got a girl now. You must respect her. No schemes or games, Trixy." I laid down the law to make sure she understood that it was business only.

"Yeah, yeah, I hear you," Trixy replied before slamming the door in my face.

Chapter 12

What Goes on in the Dark . . .
Mr. Biggs

I had been in a really bad mood for the past few weeks. Something was up and I couldn't put my finger on it. I felt like deceit was all around me. My money wasn't right and my woman was acting suspect. Not only was Maria spending more and more time with Breeze, but the other day she had the nerve to come up in my house with a dozen roses from this cat. I wasn't a man who was into beating women, but Maria's ass was coming closer and closer to bringing out the Ike Turner in me.

"Baby, let's have a candlelit dinner and a bottle of wine." Maria walked into my home office with nothing but a silk robe on.

"I'm not hungry," I said, trying to dismiss her. I had more pressing issues, like figuring out where the fuck my money was going, or why I wasn't making that much of it lately.

"Biggs, you haven't touched me in almost a week. You act like I'm not even here. What is going on?" she asked.

"It's more like what's not going on," I said, again focusing on my money instead of Maria and her complaints.

"Oh, I know what's not going on," Maria said, full of sarcasm.

"Oh, yeah, Maria? And what is that?" I said, interested in hearing what she had to say.

"You not paying me any attention. You not giving me my weekly allowance. That's a couple of things that's not going on. How about that? Shall I continue?"

"Do you have any idea why I haven't been paying you any attention or giving you an allowance, Maria?" I asked calmly.

"No, I don't, Biggs."

"Because the money coming in is getting smaller and smaller and I can't figure out why. That shit has me really stressed out." I took a sip of my cognac, then continued. "Maybe if you weren't spending so much time with Breeze you would have realized some of this," I added to let her know her actions had not gone unnoticed.

"That's my kids' father, Biggs. I have to let them see him," she replied in a low tone.

I could not believe what had just come out of her mouth. I just had to laugh. I found it funny how she went from wanting Breeze to sign over his parental rights to "that's my kids' father." For years I played daddy and took care of her kids like they were my own. For the months leading up to his release, all I heard from her was how she planned on making sure she wasn't going to let him try to come back into their lives.

I was about to remind her that she was supposed to be working on having him relinquish his parental rights, when my phone rang, saving her butt. I looked down to see Mannie's name on the screen.

"Biggs," I answered right away.

"Yo, boss, I just ran into that nigga, Breeze. I know he doing something. I think that nigga got a connect, 'cause he been making a lot of moves lately. I know he bringing in weight from somewhere. I tried to come at that nigga on some cool shit to see if he would let me in on what he been up to, but that nigga came off like we had beef or something. We gotta keep our eye on him, boss."

"Sure thing," I said before hanging up.

"Who was that on the phone?" Maria asked, full of attitude with her hands on her hips.

I didn't even bother to answer her. I knew if Breeze had a connect that could be the end of my business. I'd basically taken over the seven cities since Breeze got locked up. I was the supplier and everything went through me. If Breeze was able to get some coke just as good as mine and sell it cheaper, he could take over the streets just as quickly as he'd lost his empire. There was no way I was about to sit back and let that shit happen.

"Was that some little bitch calling for you to go see her? Huh?" Maria went on with her hands on her hips. "Answer me! Was that some whore offering you some cheap-ass pussy? Is that why you don't give me any attention anymore, Biggs? Stop ignoring me and my questions! We are not done speaking, Biggs. Our conversation is not over! Do you hear me?" she yelled as she stomped her feet like a spoiled child.

Without hesitation, I jumped out of my chair and pounced on her like a cat. "Now you listen to me, Maria! I will not be spoken to like that by anyone including you. You want an answer to your question? No, that was not some girl on the phone offering me 'cheap-ass pussy' as you wanna call it. Why would I pay for cheap pussy on the streets when I have to pay for your expensive ass here at home? Now, you will get the fuck out of my office and leave me the fuck alone. And, just so you know, shit is over when I say it's over. Do you understand me? Now get the fuck out of my office!"

She looked back at me with a bewildered look on her face, and silently walked out of the room. As far as I was concerned she knew exactly what was going on with my business. As much time as she was spending with Breeze she had to know something. I swallowed the last sip of my cognac as I sat deep in thought, formulating my next move.

Chapter 13

Money Hungry
Tanisha

Maria's evil self was in the bank as usual causing a scene because my new teller, who was helping her at the window, didn't have enough hundreds. I didn't feel like dealing with her this day, but I made sure to spend a little time with the kids before they left, and I gave them lollipops and coloring books. It was a busy Friday. The line was outside the door and cars wrapped around the drive-thru. Sara was my newbie. Her face was starting to turn red from how nervous she was, so I had to step in and help her out.

"Good morning, Mrs. Biggs and Mr. Biggs," I acknowledged them after I grabbed my vault teller to hand me a strap of hundreds. I eased in to count the money Sara was holding, and added more hundreds to make up the sum. She let out a sigh of relief when I told her I would handle the rest of the transaction.

"Always a pleasure, Tanisha," Mr. Biggs stated. Maria just crossed her arms and rolled her eyes.

"How's business?" I asked in an attempt to start a casual conversation.

"Terrible. My better half is upset because she can't have as much money today. Economy is bad so we have to tighten up," he stated, rubbing Maria's shoulder. She looked as if she despised him. I couldn't help but feel the same way about her.

Even though I would never admit it to Breeze, or anyone else for that matter, I felt jealous toward her sometimes. I knew Maria was prettier than me. Not to mention she had Breeze's kids, which meant she would always be in the picture.

"Well, Mrs. Biggs, here are your new, crisp one hundred-dollar bills. Is there anything else I can assist you with today?"

"No," Maria replied, snatching the money and putting it into an envelope herself.

At six o'clock sharp, I wrapped up and rushed out of the bank so I could be on my way to Breeze's house. I had fixed up his "bachelor pad" so it could have a warm and cozy feel to it. The best part about his place was that he had a lot of light coming through. The skylight window was perfect.

"Baby, what's up!" Breeze announced, picking me up and twirling me in the air.

"Nothing much, just another hard day at work. I'm glad it's over and the weekend is here," I said as I planted a kiss on his cheek.

"I've been busy too," he said as he put me back down. I walked toward the kitchen to grab a bottle of water.

"Hey, Tanisha," Trixy said without looking up. She was standing at the kitchen counter, counting money.

"Hi," I replied. I could tell she didn't like me; however, I just played it cool and started a visible count of the stack of money she had in her hand.

"Breeze, both of these stacks are short five hundred dollars. I got four thousand five hundred on the first one and another four thousand five hundred on the second one. Those dudes need to know how to fucking count," Trixy announced. I coughed as if I had something in my throat so Breeze could catch on. From my count, those stacks weren't short. They were both five thousand dollars even.

"Trixy, are you sure? Because lately every stack has been short. My crew can't be that fucked up," Breeze stated.

"Yeah, I'm sure, nigga," she said defensively.

"Let me count it. A second set of eyes wouldn't hurt. Breeze, maybe you should consider investing in a money counter," I suggested as I started counting money in thousand-dollar stacks. My count had been right. Both of them came out to what they was supposed to be.

"You got four thousand five hundred, right?" Trixy asked, hoping I wouldn't blow her spot up.

"No, the amount came up to ten thousand dollars not nine thousand," I insisted.

"Trixy, you stealing from me?" Breeze asked.

"Oh, so you just gonna believe her over me? You ain't gonna count it for yourself to see who's lying?" She barked at him.

"Trixy! She's a bank manager. She counts money for a living. Why the fuck wouldn't I believe her over your ass? How you gonna do me like that, Trixy?" he asked with anger in his voice.

"Because, nigga! I was the only woman who gave a damn about you when you came home. You ain't have shit when I took you in and the second you got some paper you played me! You didn't look out for me. Instead you went and got you a snooty-ass, uppity bitch who probably don't give a fuck about you, anyway. Maria left your ass to rot in prison and this bitch will do the same shit!" Trixy proclaimed.

"Man, roll the fuck out. I won't be needing you anymore. Go suck some dick so you can get your cable bill paid this month. You messed up a good thing, Trixy," Breeze yelled, now in a rage.

"Fuck you, Breeze," Trixy responded before throwing a pile of money in his face.

"Bitch, get the fuck out my house before I stomp your face in! You lucky I ain't fucking you up for messing with my paper," Breeze spat at her as he practically kicked her out the door.

I didn't know what to make of the way he had just yelled at Trixy. I almost felt sorry for the girl. I understood she was stealing from him but that was really harsh. I didn't even know he was capable of speaking to someone like that. It dawned on me that there was a side to Breeze that I had not been exposed to: a cold, ruthless side. I was fully aware that I was dealing with a drug dealer, but he acted like such a gentleman with me. He treated me like a queen. I must admit, seeing that side of him scared me a little bit, but on the other hand, it gave me reassurance that he knew how to handle himself if something ever happened.

Chapter 14

Payback
Trixy

This nigga was trying to play me over some snooty-ass bitch who didn't even want him. I bet if his ass got in a jam again, he would have tried to creep back up into my bed again. I knew I wasn't the first or the last to dip in the pot. It's just how the game goes. I had been counting money and moving shit for Breeze for a while, and this was the motherfucking thanks I got. Niggas fucked him over and he had to come back to me. It had been proven that I was the only person who truly had his back. Breeze had fucked me over for the last time. It was time he paid. I guess that nigga had forgotten I was from the streets too. No one fucked with me and got away with it. Sure, I left Breeze's spot without a fight, but I left my mark before leaving. On the way to my car, I couldn't help but notice a hefty tree branch on the side of the curb. I happily picked it up and busted Breeze's and Tanisha's windows out of their cars.

"Who's laughing now?" I shouted as I sped off. "Payback's a bitch! I got something for your ass, nigga. The sun won't rise in the morning, fool," I ranted to myself as I drove toward Park Place, going seventy-five miles per hour.

I found Mannie at the barber shop, gambling as usual. I walked right up in the middle of the game. "Hey, Mannie, you got a minute?"

"Damn, Trixy, what the fuck?" Mannie looked up at me with a snarl on his face.

"We need to talk. On the real!" I snapped.

"Come with me. I was about to roll out anyway." Mannie knew it must have been something serious.

I hopped in the car and we headed to his favorite strip club. It was a hole in the wall, a little place called Dexter's in Portsmouth. We walked in and found a secluded seat in the corner of the little smoke-infested place. We weren't there five minutes before some old-ass man had the nerve to come over and ask me if I was going to get my ass on the sticky pole. I took a deep breath in an attempt to maintain my composure. I was already pissed the hell off. The last thing I wanted to do was come off on this old man like a psycho bitch.

"No, sir, I'm not a dancer," I said calmly.

"Well, you shole is pretty enough. Girl, you got a whole lotta junk in your trunk," he said between missing teeth like the character Jerome from the sitcom *Martin*.

Once the old man walked away, I dove right into conversation with Mannie. "Breeze has been playing you. He's trying to take over this whole area and put you out of business. At first he was taking birds from you, cooking them up and breaking it down, then sending it to some cats across town. Then he hooked up with this Mexican in California and now he's pushing weight. He got purer coke for a cheaper price. The fucked-up thing is he wouldn't work with you because he wasn't trying to do all the work while you make the money, in turn making Mr. Biggs rich. Mannie, this nigga has plans to take over the whole seven cities. He trying to lock it down like he had it before he got locked up."

"Oh, yeah? So what make you come with this news?" Mannie questioned my motives.

"Damn, Mannie. You know we go way back. You my nigga. I always look out for mines. I hate

to bring you bad news, but I felt you needed to
know what's about to pop off. You know my loyalty always lies with you. Plus, I heard Mr. Biggs
been getting some losses because of this shit.
Don't y'all niggas wanna know where the lack of
business is coming from? I know you didn't think
it was because of the recession. Ain't no fucking
recession in the drug game. Just droughts and
losses!" I spat.

"The streets talk, baby girl. Nigga knew something was up. We were just waiting to see what
was really going on." Mannie didn't say much,
but I knew from the look on his face it was time
for war.

"This nigga just got out of prison. Now he's
trying to be the king. Breeze even trying to bring
niggas from New York to start taking over the
blocks." I added fuel to the fire.

"A'ight. Thanks for looking out for me, Trixy.
Here's some paper for you," he said, breaking
me off a couple hundreds. "Keep looking out
like that and I got you, shorty. Just let me know
what's up."

"No problem. It's getting late. I need to get
going," I replied. I quickly took the money and
left. I didn't want Mannie to see the tears running down my face. The truth was that I really

was feeling Breeze, maybe even loved him. Even worse, he was my son's father. That's right, I got pregnant on the first fuck. That nigga was so happy to be in virgin pussy that he didn't even bother to wear a condom. Then he told my little naive ass that a virgin couldn't get pregnant on the first fuck. But what do you know? Trixy ends up pregnant and no sooner than I find out does he go to jail. Besides, I knew there was no chance in hell that the almighty street king, Breeze, would claim a baby from a hood rat like me. I'd raised my child alone for six years and I was prepared to continue with or without Breeze. Stupid-ass nigga never even asked who my son was a junior to. Maybe if he would have asked, he would know he was the senior to my junior.

Payback was a bitch, and it was time Breeze learned it. He had to learn I wasn't some jump-off bitch he could just toss away. After I got into the car, I started punching the steering wheel, imagining it was Breeze's face.

Chapter 15

Word on the Street
Mr. Biggs

The sound of my phone during dinner really burned me up.

"This better be good," I said as soon as I picked up.

"Oh, it is," Mannie vowed. "I just got word on Breeze. That nigga has a connect with the Mexicans. He's definitely been taking our business. He been flooding the seven cities with better coke at cheaper prices. That's why we can't compete. From what I hear, he's got plans to take over." Mannie ran down the information like a confidential informant working for the police.

"Nobody's gonna take what I have and I'll make sure of that. I knew this day was soon coming. I've thought long and hard about it. I already have a plan in mind. I know what I have to do.

I'm gonna make some phone calls and get back to you. Get ready for war, Mannie. Be ready to go on the word," I directed him.

"You got it, boss. I'ma spread the word we shot shit to do," he said before hanging up.

"Damn it!" I yelled as I threw my glass of wine against the wall.

"Biggs! Have you lost your mind? You're scaring the children," Maria yelled, then directed her attention toward the kids. "You guys may be excused. Go on and get ready for your baths." She sent them away from the dinner table. I completely ignored her as I dialed up Li'l D.

"What up boss?" he answered on the second ring.

"It's time for war."

"I'm ready. When and where?" Li'l D asked like the true soldier he was.

"It's Breeze. We gotta let this nigga know we mean business. Find out where his spot is and run up in there. Round up the soldiers and hit him late in the night tomorrow," I instructed Li'l D.

"Done," D said before hanging up. I felt a little more at ease after getting off the phone with him. I knew if I could count on anyone to get the job done, it was Li'l D. He was what you call a true soldier; he didn't ask questions and just did as instructed.

"What is that all about?" Maria was in my face before I could even put my phone down on the table. This woman was really starting to get on my last nerve.

"Get out of my face, Maria. This doesn't concern you," I warned her.

"No!" she yelled, then proceeded to put her finger in my face. "You will tell me what is going on!"

Without warning, I jumped out of the chair and pushed Maria against the wall. While pinned against the wall, I grabbed her by the neck and whispered in her ear, "This does not concern you," then I walked away.

Chapter 16

Women of My Life
Breeze

"May I take your order, please?" the waitress asked Tanisha. I could tell she hadn't been in good spirits all day.

"I'll have your sliced tomato and onion salad and a glass of merlot. That's all for me," Tanisha replied.

"All right, and for you, sir."

"Let me get the steak and lobster tail. For my steak, I would like it to be cooked well done. Also, I want a cold glass of Heineken."

"No problem," the waitress responded after jotting down our order and taking the menus from us.

"Baby, what's going on? What's on your mind?" I asked, truly concerned.

"I'm fine," Tanisha commented.

"No, you're not. Something is going on. Is it me?"

"It's nothing like that. Breeze, I have to tell you something."

"What is it? You can talk to me about anything, Tanisha," I assured her.

"Well, it's just that every man dreams of a beautiful wife and kids. I'm confident that I could be the perfect wife for you, but it's the children who are a problem."

"What? Are you saying you don't want to have my children?" I asked.

"No. I'm not saying that at all. I would love to have your children Breeze. It's that I can't." She said with a worried look.

"Why not? Is it because of the drug game? Tanisha, I promise you this is all just temporary," I explained.

"Breeze, listen to me," Tanisha said sternly, then paused. She took a sip of her water, took a deep breath, and then continued. "I can't have babies. I don't ovulate as a normal woman would." She broke down sobbing.

I quickly grabbed the cloth napkin that set on the table. "Take this," I offered.

"Thanks," she whispered.

"I'm so sorry, Tanisha," I added, caressing her hand.

"When the doctor told me on my last visit, I was speechless. The doctor said my eggs are not strong enough to conceive, let alone carry a baby to full term. I've always wanted a big family. Now I feel like I'm less than a woman."

"I hear you. Listen, if it will help, the next time I get the kids, you can join us."

"Okay," she agreed.

"Cheer up, babe. Maybe, if you're willing, we can look into going to a specialist or something. I hear all the time about woman having children by surrogate moms. Don't worry. We'll work something out." I tried my best to console her.

The rest of our dinner was kind of quiet and awkward. All sorts of things were going through my mind, but I tried not to show any worry across my face. After we ate, I grabbed a couple of DVDs from the Redbox at the store, and we headed home.

While we were in the middle of one of the movies Tanisha said, "Thank you for being there for me." Since we had come home, I'd been doing my best to be a little extra affectionate with her hoping to get her to feel a little better about her situation. She was sitting between my legs, and we were hugged up under a blanket. I was doing my best to get through it, but that food from Ruth's Chris was starting to put me to sleep.

"You're welcome. That's what I'm here for," I said before yawning.

"Listen, it's getting late and I have to be to work at seven o'clock in the morning for a manager's meeting. Before I go, I want you to know I really appreciate you being so supportive about this whole thing. It makes me feel so much better that you are okay with me not being able to have children. I was so scared of how you were going to react to the news," Tanisha explained as she turned her face to look at me.

"Why would you be scared? I got you, baby. I ain't going nowhere," I said as I leaned in to kiss her forehead. I pulled away, and she turned herself all the way around. She gave me soft, sweet kisses as her hands gently ran down my stomach and landed on the zipper of my jeans.

I allowed Tanisha to take the lead. Sex with her was different from the usual rough sex I had with Trixy. It was always deep and passionate. Whenever we had sex, I never got the urge to just want to bang her out and get my nut. With her, I would usually take my time and explore her body. I don't know what it was about her that wouldn't get me to just want to fuck her like that. The weird part was that I didn't even miss the rough sex, and I was cool with it.

After unzipping my jeans, she pulled them, along with my boxers, off. She took her time gripping my dick with both her hands. Then she looked up at me with a devilish smirk as she began to trace swirls with her tongue around the head of my penis. After that, she bent her head over and started sucking and kissing it all around. My shit started getting real wet and all her extra spit was dripping all over my balls. I don't know how or where she learned to be so on point with her head game. You'd never expect to get such good head from a classy-type woman. Either way, I was loving the shit out of it. When my balls were dripping wet, she grabbed one with each hand and began massaging them while she sucked on the tip of my dick. After a couple of minutes she got up and started stripping in front of me. Damn, this girl was sexy. My dick stood rock hard as she pulled off her clothes and straddled me. She sat down on top of me and slid my dick inside her. Her pussy was so tight, and it felt extra good that she let me go in raw dog. I guess she didn't mind not using a condom since she couldn't get pregnant anyway. Tanisha squeezed my nipples as she rode me giving long, deep strokes, forcing my dick deeper and deeper inside her. I could have busted off just from the moans and groans she made. And, I gotta admit, it'd been a long time since I had straight skin-to-skin contact, so my shit was feeling extra sensitive right about now. We made sweet love for thirty minutes before we came together.

After Tanisha left, I was already starting to miss her when my phone rang.

"Hello?" I answered.

"Um, hey, Breeze, it's Maria. I'm sorry to be calling so late. Would it be all right if the kids and I come over for a bit?" Maria asked in a low, cracked voice. I wasn't sure, but it almost sounded like she was crying.

"Yeah, that's cool. Is everything straight wit'chu? Are my kids okay?" I asked. Maria had never asked to come over, and she had never called so late. I knew something was up.

"Yes."

"Do you know where the Hamptons Apartments are?" I asked.

"It's near the water, right?"

"Yeah, it's apartment number five. I'll see you when you get here."

I paced the floor and kept looking at the clock while I waited for Maria to reach me. It seemed like every five minutes I would look out the window, hoping to see them walking up. I couldn't relax. I felt deep inside that something was wrong. All I could think about was that that Mr. Biggs nigga had done something to my kids. My mind was made up; if that nigga had touched my kids I would be going back to prison. I knew that would be well worth the trip. I would spend the rest of my life in jail or go to the electric chair to protect my children.

When I looked out the window for the fourth time I saw Maria and the children. I quickly ran to the door and swung it open. After the kids came through the front door, I scooped them both up at the same time for hugs. Maria didn't say much, but I could see worry all over her face. I didn't want to talk about things in front of the kids, so I turned on the TV and grabbed some snacks. With popcorn and grape soda in our hands, we watched about thirty minutes of *The Proud Family*. It didn't take long before they were knocked out. After I laid them down on my bed and made sure they were comfortable, I came back to the living room to chat with Maria.

"What's going on? Maria, you didn't come over tonight for nothing."

"Biggs slammed me up against the wall," she explained, showing me the bruises on her back. She kept her face down, and I could tell she was embarrassed about it.

"Is this the first time? Did he do it in front of my kids?" I asked, more concerned about my kids' safety than Maria's bruises.

"No, he didn't do it in front of them. Yes, it was his first time. He's frustrated about the business. Money is barely coming in. From what I hear, he thinks you're trying to take over his empire. Breeze, watch your back. Biggs, Li'l D, Mannie, and their little goons may be paying you a visit," she added before getting up and almost slipping on some soda the kids had spilt earlier. I reached out and caught her in my arms just in time.

"You okay?" I asked, smirking. Call me messed up, but it took everything in me not to laugh at the way she almost busted her ass.

"Yeah, I'm okay, thanks," she said as she looked up at me.

"Good, 'cause that shit would've been real funny if you woulda fallen!" I said. I couldn't hold it back anymore and fell out laughing.

"Breeze! You never change!" she said in between laughs. "Boy, you so stupid!" she said, doing her best Gina impersonation from *Martin*.

"Oh, wow! You taking it real back with that one, Maria. I forgot all about that," I said to her. Back when we were dating, we used to watch *Martin* every night it came on. She and I had this thing where I would be her Martin and she would be my Gina. Seeing her do that reminded me of the Maria I'd fallen in love with so many years back. When we finally calmed down from laughing, there was an awkward silence between us. I let go of her and was about to walk away, when she grabbed my arm to stop me.

"Breeze, I'm sorry for everything I've done to you," Maria confessed, "I know it probably doesn't make that much of a difference, but I really mean it. I was wrong for a lot of things."

"Maria, you will never know how bad you hurt me," was all I could respond at that moment. I didn't know what to make of her apology. I never expected that to come out of her mouth. As long as I'd known her, she had always been too proud to admit to anybody if she was ever wrong about something.

Our eyes met and we started kissing. The more we kissed, the more my feelings took me

back to when we were married. Now, I had her
pinned up against the wall. Not wanting to hurt
her back any more than it already was, I spun
her around and pushed her breasts up against
the wall. I kissed her neck while I rubbed my
hands along her waist and thighs. I hadn't been
this physically close to her in years and she felt
so unbelievably good. I lifted her summer dress
up and moved her panties to the side. I had been
waiting five long years for this moment. I slid
two fingers in her slit and started rotating my
fingers.

"Breeze," she moaned in between breaths.
"Oh, Breezy. Give it to me," she whispered and
moaned.

"Remember this?" I asked as I eased my dick
into her pussy. I almost lost my breath when I
pushed every inch of myself all the way in one
swift motion. I grabbed her by the hips and wasted no time getting in some deep, long strokes.
No one could ever take my strokes like that
except for Maria. Nigga felt like he was finally
home while being up in there.

"Yes." She shuddered in ecstasy. I began caressing her nipples just the way she'd always
liked it. Some things about Maria I could just
never forget. She began to tighten her pussy

around my dick. As she pushed her head back, Maria closed her eyes, enjoying this pleasure I was giving to her. I came without a moment's notice and so did she.

As soon as I came, I felt guilty about what I had just done. She pulled her dress back down and asked where the bathroom was so she could freshen up. As I stood there getting myself together, my mind was everywhere. I was used to fucking with different women all the time, but tonight was different. I had just fucked my wife hours within having made love to wifey. But what fucked me up right now was that I felt like I'd just cheated Tanisha and not Maria. Maria was my wife and my kids' mother, but she wasn't about shit. Yeah, she'd said she was sorry, but I wasn't fazed or moved by her comments. The way I saw it, she saw me on the come up again, and realized that her man was going down, so she wanted to make sure she stayed on the winner's side. I knew deep inside she didn't give a damn about anyone but herself and money. She probably figured I would just open my arms and take her back like it was all water under the bridge, but she had another thing coming. Even with that said, I let Maria and the kids stay at my place for the night.

The next morning, I got Maria and the kids up early. I had some business to take care of and I wanted them out of the house. Before sending them off, I gave Maria a cell phone so that I could reach her and the kids at all times.

As soon as they left, I started making some phone calls. Before noon hit, I had my soldiers gathered up and ready to go. We paid Mannie a little visit, announcing our arrival by blasting his door wide open. I had to let these niggas know we meant business. Borne and one of his boys took to the left while me and two of my other niggas went right. Motherfuckers didn't know what hit them. There were a couple of hoes in there sucking dick, so we got to see some titties bouncing while we handled our business. After we made sure we had left our mark, we casually walked out of the house like nothing had happened.

"Good shit," I said to Borne as we sat at a diner having lunch. "I'm glad I got to them before they got to me," I added.

"Yeah nigga. These motherfuckers need to recognize shit is about to change, 'cause we taking back over!" he said as he reached over to give me a pound.

"Yeah!" I chuckled. "I'm just mad that nigga Mannie had been there for the party," I said. We finished our plates and I went back to the bachelor pad. I knew once the word spread about what had happened, Biggs was really gonna have it out for me, so I had to lay low for a while. I rounded up a few im-portant things and set off to a hotel in Williamsburg. My next step was to get another spot no one would know about.

"Ah, man," I sighed while lying across the bed. I looked at the phone to see I'd just missed Tanisha's call. I didn't call her back because I really wasn't in the mood for talking. Besides, I couldn't dare tell her what happened. My baby was a worrywart, and I didn't want to add more to her daily stress.

Seconds later the phone rang again. This time it was Maria. All fucking day Maria had been blowing me up from the cell phone I gave her when she came over. I assumed Mr. Biggs still didn't know about it. Otherwise, the phone would have definitely been cut off. I was hoping she wasn't about to start off on some baby momma drama level. You know how it usually goes: you give your baby mother a little bit of leeway and she goes psycho on you. When I gave her the phone I specifically told her the phone was so I could get in contact with my kids, but the way she was calling, it was more like the other way around. She finally texted me, saying that the kids wanted to talk to me. The first thing that came to mind was that she hadn't been letting me talk to my kids since I came out, but now, all of a sudden, I was that important. I was definitely not in the mood for playing any of her dumbass games, but I called anyway.

"Hello?" I asked.

"Do have any idea how long I have been calling trying to reach you?" Maria shouted so loud it hurt my ear.

"Yeah. Where are the kids?" I said nonchalantly.

"So that's the only reason you called back? I've been blowing you up all day, Breeze," Maria continued to shout.

"Maria, if you have been calling me all day to argue, then I'm out. I've had a long, hard fucking day and I'm not in the mood for this shit," I explained to her.

"No, I didn't call to argue. I have to tell you something."

"Go ahead," I said.

"I lied."

"You lied about what, Maria?" I said, sounding a little annoyed.

"I lied about the house. The truth is I never sold it. I just relayed that tidbit of information to your mother because I couldn't stand her and I wanted to hurt you. Now that that's out the way, let me get to the point. I know a little bit about what's going on and I want to help you."

"What did you hear?" I curiously asked.

"You're in danger. Biggs has a fifty thousand dollar hit on you."

"Hmm," I replied, trying my best to show no emotion.

"The house is yours. It's still fully furnished. No one would expect you to be there because everybody thinks I sold it. I put the key in the old post office box we set up by Indian River Road. All you have to do is pull it open gently because the door is unlocked," she added.

"A'ight. I will take care of that. Now, let me talk to my kids," I ordered.

"One last thing I have to say," she insisted.

"What?" Now she was really starting to aggravate me.

"I never stopped thinking about you. Breeze, you left me and I just didn't know how to deal with it. You will always have my heart," she said, sounding sincere. I wanted to believe Maria but I couldn't help but feel as if she had an ulterior motive. There was too much stuff that wasn't adding up, and history had already proved she was not to be trusted.

"Okay. Thanks, Maria," was all I replied.

"That's all you have to say back, Breeze? Really?" she asked with confusion, surprise, and a little bit of hurt combined in her tone of voice.

"Are the kids coming to the phone?" I replied, ignoring her questions.

"Hold on," was all she said, but not before sucking her teeth loud enough for me to hear.

Chapter 17

Baby Momma Drama
Tanisha

Wow, Breeze's house should be classified as a castle, I thought as he showed me around. It had a spacious kitchen with a full breakfast bar and an island with a customized stove top. The cabinets were made from dark cherry wood with frosted glass and silver knobs, which complemented to perfection the stainless steel appliances and granite countertops. All together, there were six bedrooms and four full bathrooms. The master bedroom had a beautiful fireplace and private balcony that overlooked an eight-foot deep pool with Jacuzzi. The house also included an attached three-car garage, with a gym, and, as if that were not enough, it also had a family room and separate playroom for the kids. Not to mention, each room had customized crown molding.

I couldn't believe Breeze had purchased that house with drug money. Call me naive, but I'd never seen drug money on such a level. Breeze was definitely reaping the fruits of his labor. I couldn't help but pray that being back in his old house wouldn't encourage him to want to stay in the game longer than planned. Breeze assured me that his house was paid for, so I figured we would be fine with my income and him establishing his own business to have on the side. I just had to sit down with him and discuss exactly what kind of business he wanted to look into. Honestly, I couldn't see Breeze working for someone else for the rest of his life. He just didn't take well to authority.

"So how do you like the house?" he asked, eagerly waiting for my answer.

"Like? Honey, I adore the house. It's exquisite," I replied with a peck on his lips. Then we headed toward the playroom, where we found the kids busy playing a Nintendo Wii game.

"Kids, I fixed up your rooms," Breeze called out to them. I smiled when I heard them giggling and laughing as they made their way toward us.

"Great," they replied in unison, giving him a hug. Then, to my pleasant surprise, they turned to hug me as well. I must admit it felt a little weird to be around them. Up until today, the only time I had ever seen them was when they came in with Maria at the bank. Having them around more often was definitely something I was looking forward to.

"Um, Dad, is Ms. Tanisha going to be our new mommy like we have a new daddy?" Jaden asked Breeze.

"Actually, that's one of the things I wanted to talk about with you and your sister. Ms. Tanisha is going to be your stepmother after she and I get married. There are some things I need to explain to you two first. Now, let's start by talking about this whole daddy thing." Breeze stooped down so that he was at eye level with the children. Then he grabbed their hands as he spoke. "Kids, I need you to understand that you only have one daddy," Breeze began to say, but was interrupted by a strange noise. "What's that noise coming from outside?" he said to no one in particular, then quickly clicked on the surveillance camera that showed views from every angle on the outside of the house as well as inside. Breeze seemed a little on edge to me, but I didn't bother saying anything.

"Dad, it's the ice cream truck! Can we have some please, Daddy," Kaylyn replied excitedly.

After zooming in on the front gate camera and confirming she was right, Breeze gave the kids the okay to get some ice cream. "Here's some money," he said, handing Jaden a twenty-dollar bill.

"Thanks." Kaylyn giggled and the kids ran off.

"Did you want anything?" Breeze asked me.

"No, I'm fine. Aren't you going to get something?" I asked in return.

"You know the only sweet I'm into is your pussy," he whispered into my ear.

"I second that notion and the one where I'll be the proud stepmother; however, first, you need to get a divorce. According to my book of law, you can only have one wife," I explained.

"I'm taking care of that." Breeze assured me with a kiss.

"All right." I nodded.

"Since the kids are outside, I have one more room to show you," he mentioned, leading the way.

We walked through the master bedroom and he led me to the walk-in closet. Breeze hit a button on the wall and the shelves spread apart, showing a door. We opened the door and headed down some stairs. As we inched closer to this special room, I was hoping it would be a romantic room that only we would know about. To my disappointment, it looked more liked a fixed-up energy-efficient apartment equipped with a bedroom, bathroom, phone, mini kitchen, and two flat-screen televisions.

"What is this?" I asked, confused.

"It's a panic room. If any of us are ever in danger, we can come down here. It's resistant to bullets. The door is made of steel and has a lock release. Unless someone blows it up, they're not getting it open," Breeze explained.

"Let's hope we never have to use this room," I said, a little concerned Breeze would have need for such a room. Instantly, thoughts of Jose came into my head, causing my stomach to turn.

"I'll hope for the best, but prepare for the worst. All that matters to me is you and the kids and y'all safety. Matter of fact, pack your bags. You're off for a few days, so I figured we could go to Atlanta to do a little shopping, and maybe while we're there we can take the kids to the zoo and the aquarium. I already spoke to Maria about taking the kids on vacation for a couple of days with me, so everything is all set to go," Breeze directed.

***

We had a wonderful weekend, and Monday came around before I knew it. My days off flew by so fast, and I was back to my normal routine at work. I was grateful that I had scheduled myself to work the late shift that day, because I did not have the energy to go in early in the morning. Unfortunately, it had completely slipped my mind that the late shift would require me to have to deal with Maria's weekly Monday visit. I opened my office door and noticed that only Maria and the kids were here today. I found it a little unusual that Mr. Biggs wasn't with them. The kids ran up to me, and gave me hugs with sticky lollipop juice dripping all over their hands. I wondered if the kids had told Maria about me being their stepmother, or that I had been with them the entire time they were with their father over the weekend. As I looked up at her, I couldn't tell if she was upset from the expression on her face, because she always looked at me nasty.

"I've been waiting for you. Kids, go sit at the coloring table," she ordered them.

"Hello. What can I help you with this afternoon?" I asked in my most professional voice.

"Bitch, I always knew you wanted Biggs but you went as far as fucking my husband, Breeze? Let me make something clear to you, sweetie. Both of those men belong to me. They both are mine. Breeze is just passing the time with you." She spat at me, "Did he tell you that house you've been in all weekend is the house that we shared together? Damn, Tanisha, I didn't take you for the type to take another woman's leftovers," she growled at me.

I could not believe this woman had the nerve to come to my job to bring personal drama. I knew this moment would happen eventually, but I would have thought she would have had the decency to at least do it somewhere else. None-theless, I refused to stoop to this woman's level. "Let's get one thing straight. I do not nor have I ever wanted anything to do with Mr. Biggs, and I do not intend on stealing anyone's husband. If these men 'belong to you' as you stated earlier, then I suggest you speak with them about all of that because I refuse to stand here discussing my personal life with you. Moving on, one thing I do need to speak with you about is the fact that all of your accounts are overdrawn at this time. Now, as the bank manager I must inform you that we will be adding overdraft fees to any additional charges added to these accounts until they are brought back to a positive status. Now, if these accounts are not restored within twenty-four to fourty-eight hours, I will be forced to freeze them. Do you have any questions, *Mrs. Biggs*?" I asked with a smug look on my face. It felt so good to have the opportunity to say all this to such a snooty, high-and-mighty woman like herself.

"Bitch, I will not have you speak to me like that. Do you have any idea how much money we have invested in this bank in the past?" Maria yelled, and slapped me across the face.

The devil in me wanted to grab Maria by the hair and throw her across the room, but the Southern beauty in me stayed calm. Instead, I quickly called security. Thankfully, the kids hadn't seen the commotion. Within seconds, security kindly walked Maria out of the bank. I was so pissed that I left for the rest of the day. I didn't need this type of crap in my place of employment. Banks don't like drama. They have too much of an image to uphold.

I couldn't dial Breeze's number fast enough as I walked to my car.

"Talk to me," Breeze answered the phone.

"Maria came to the bank and slapped me. Breeze, I have never gone through anything like this before in my life! You better get control of her, now, before I send her to jail. I'm not going to put up with this crap! Oh, and by the way, you could have told me that was the house you had with her. I don't like to be in the dark about certain things," I said, and hung the phone up on him. I decided to go to my mother's house to cool down. Breeze quickly called back but I just turned my phone off. For one day, I just didn't want to deal with it.

Chapter 18

Setting Boundaries
Breeze

My head was pounding as I kept dialing Maria's cell phone number and continued to pace the floor. *Who does this bitch think she is? When we was together at first, I cared so much about impressing her, the snobby parents, and her snotty-ass friends. The irony is Maria is just as bad as any other average ghetto bitch.*

I wish she had given me her house phone number because I would have called that number too. Knowing Maria, her ass was probably laughing at me, hoping Tanisha would have left me by now. I couldn't blame Tanisha for not wanting to get into a whole bunch of drama. She was right. I should have told her about the damn house. That way, Maria wouldn't have been able to throw that shit in her face. Deep down, I knew

a real woman like Tanisha didn't want to feel like
as if she was taking second place. At this point, I
still hadn't been able to get through to Tanisha.
I tried calling, but I couldn't get a hold of her,
either. Worst of all, I didn't know if Maria had
told her about us having sex. I knew I couldn't
put nothing past Maria's conniving ass. That
bitch just couldn't stand to see me happy. What I
couldn't believe was that she had actually put her
hands on my woman.

"Hello?" Maria finally answered in tears.

"Now you finally want to pick up the phone,"
I snapped.

"Biggs hit me again. He thinks there's somebody else because I won't sleep with him anymore," she said between tears.

"Bitch, if I had his number I'd tell him myself that I fucked you the other night. Shit, who
knows how many other niggas you been fuckin'
lately. I mean, it shouldn't be that hard to figure
it out. Just see what dudes are making the most
money. You all about the dollars, right? Your
pussy goes where the money goes. So I guess that
makes you a ho. Matter of fact, tell that nigga to
smack you again for me," I shouted. I couldn't
give a fuck about Maria getting smacked. She
had truly crossed the line this time.

"What? Breeze, how could you talk to me like this? The only person I've slept with is you. I put that on my kids," Maria vowed.

There was no way I could believe anything Maria said anymore. Deep inside I knew Maria wasn't the ho type, but I also knew she was all about the dollars. On the real, that was probably the only reason she even slept with me. She saw the money leaving Biggs and coming to me. I knew if a chick was that crazy about money anything was possible. I couldn't put nothing past Maria.

"Whatever, Maria, save it, please. That's not even important to me right now. I've been calling you about a more pressing issue. Now listen to me and listen to me closely. Stay the hell away from Tanisha. She ain't got shit to do with me and you," I demanded.

"Breeze, I'm sorry. Baby, please forgive me. It's just that I've never thought about you being with anyone else. Then to find out about Tanisha, it killed me inside. I've been thinking about getting our family back together. The kids love you so much and I'm starting to fall back in love with you all over again. Please, Breeze, we can work this out," Maria begged.

"Maria, you're wasting your breath."

"Baby, just give me another chance to prove to you that I won't leave you ever again."

"Maria, please," I shouted to get her attention. Her begging was really starting to get under my skin. "You're becoming borderline pathetic. We ain't ever getting back together. I don't want you. In fact, I plan to marry Tanisha. I'll be drawing up divorce papers real soon."

"Not so fast. We had sex, which means I get another year of convincing you to stay with your true family," Maria stated as if she where some sort of divorce attorney. I had to wonder if she'd planned this all along.

"What judge is going to believe you slept with me? Remember, I'm the convict you deserted in prison. You been moved on now to Mr. Biggs, who definitely ain't going to go for that. I've always told your dumb ass, Maria, to think before you speak."

"Fuck you, Breeze, you won't marry that bitch, and you won't see your kids again, either. I'm gonna make sure of that!" Maria announced, and hung up the phone.

I kept calling back, but I continued to get her voice mail. Even though I wanted to, I didn't leave a voice message or text because I didn't

want her to come back and say I was harassing
her. There was no telling what Maria was capable of. I wouldn't have been surprised if she
tried to pin her battered bruises on me so I could
go back and sit in a prison cell.

Chapter 19

Going In
Mr. Biggs

"Hey, baby." Maria walked in the room in sexy lingerie.

"Hey, honey," I responded, not giving much attention to her.

"I know money and work have been stressing you out lately." She began to massage my shoulders. "So I have a little bit of information that you may want to hear."

"And what is that, Maria?" She finally had my attention. I was interested to hear just how much information Maria could provide that would actually help my financial situation.

"I know where Breeze is," she whispered in my ear.

"Oh, yeah?" I said, knowing that was no fucking surprise.

"Yes, sir. He's staying in Virginia Beach near the courthouse. I can give you the address."

"And how did you get this information?" I asked just for fun. I knew exactly how Maria knew, but I was curious how she would answer.

"I've been dropping the kids off there to visit. It looks like he's making a lot of money, Biggs. You should see the size of the house he lives in. You know, I wouldn't be surprised if his come up is the cause of your money losses," Maria added.

I didn't say anything as she spoke. It was amazing how Maria really thought she was manipulating me. She had no idea that I knew everything she did. I wondered at that point if I should tell her I knew this house she was speaking of was the house she and Breeze used to live in. Not to mention this same house had supposedly been sold.

"Baby, I think it's time you showed Breeze you mean business. He's gotten away with too much. Besides, our family is suffering. You and the boys should pay him a little visit. I don't want anyone to get hurt; just shake him up a little bit. This time you guys will definitely come out on top. I'm sure he's there relaxing, thinking he's safe."

"I wonder what would make a woman turn on a man so quickly," I said to her, insinuating that there must be something more she's not telling me. I wanted to know Maria's motivation.

"Baby, I hate seeing you like this. You're always on edge and we are constantly fighting. You don't even touch me anymore. I just want you happy. I want our relationship back." Maria almost sounded sincere.

"Thanks for the information. Guess it's time I show everyone I mean business," I said, knowing that, in the end, it wouldn't be just Breeze who felt that wrath.

Chapter 20

Last Breath
Tanisha

After a lot of convincing from him, Breeze and I spent a quiet weekend in Richmond. He brought me up to speed on everything. I mean, this man poured his whole heart out to me. It was a lot to take in. Now, worry and uncertainty had really settled in my heart for him and his children. It had been proven that Maria was a loose cannon.

I struggled with myself on what to do. *Can I really deal with this? A small part of me feels I should leave. Hell, my life could be in danger. Meanwhile, Mr. Biggs still comes in the bank every week, smiling in my face, knowing damn well I'm Breeze's lady.* Breeze got on his knees and begged me to stay. Deep down, I truly loved this man. I had to wonder if I was willing to gamble my heart for him.

"I loved that movie," the kids expressed after watching *The Princess and The Frog*. We had just gotten back from Busch Gardens. I figured letting them watch a movie would settle them down so they would go to bed. Breeze loaded them up with way too much sugar while we were at the park. After eating snow cones and funnel cakes all day, my teeth started hurting.

"Tanisha, can you come in the kitchen, please?" Breeze asked.

"Okay," I responded, leaving the kids in the living room.

"Wow, I didn't even hear you come downstairs," I stated. Breeze was pacing back and forth.

"They're coming for me," he replied in a low voice.

"Who?"

"Tanisha, now isn't the time. You know who's coming. We talked about the worst-case scenario. Well, it's happening now. Take this gun and take the kids to the panic room. Remember, don't open the door unless I say our code word: grapes," he instructed.

"I don't know how to use a gun," I responded with fear.

"Just aim and shoot. We don't have much time. I can see them beginning to surrounded the house. I guess they waiting for us to turn the lights out. Meanwhile, I put clothes and food down there just in case. The kids are sleepy so hopefully they won't hear a thing. I love you," he replied.

"I love you too," I said before kissing him. I quickly moved the kids down to the panic room and locked the door. My eyes were fixated on what the security cameras showed. I began hearing shots fired from all different directions. Breeze was handling his gunfire with these men who appeared to look like black ninjas. A few minutes, which seemed like hours, passed. It was so quiet that I could have heard a pin drop. Suddenly, I saw someone get into Breeze's car and speed off; but I couldn't tell if it was him or the culprits.

The police sirens were coming closer. I was silently praying that Breeze wasn't dead. I left the kids in the panic room with cartoons on. They were drifting in and out of sleep and had no idea what was really going on. I slowly crept upstairs so I could see if anyone was still in the house. These voices were coming closer; I hid in our bedroom closet and I cracked the closet door open.

It was none other than Mr. Biggs and Maria. He had a gun to Maria's chest.

"Please, Biggs. What are you doing? You promised no one would get hurt," Maria cried frantically.

"You worthless, cheating, money-hungry bitch. Don't tell me what the fuck to do. I gave you everything. All I wanted in return was your loyalty. If your greed would set Breeze up to die, then your greed would do it to me too. I'm not dying for a whore like you. That nigga ain't been out a year and you already fucking him. Maria, people talk. Besides, I had a private investigator on your ass the whole time," he said, flinging pictures on the bed.

Biggs shot Maria in the chest and simply left. Once I heard the front door open and close, I came out of the closet. Shortly after, the police entered the house. One officer called for an ambulance.

"The paramedics are on the way," I told Maria while compressing the wound on her chest with some clothes I'd grabbed in order to stop the bleeding.

"Where are my babies?" she asked, barely able to breathe.

"They're safe," I assured her.

"Biggs shot me. All of this is my fault. I told Biggs everything about Breeze and his business because I wanted to get back at him. Biggs promised me no one would get hurt. He was only supposed to rob Breeze and scare him a little. I didn't expect things to end this way. Tell my kids that Mommy loves her sugar babies. They'll know what it means. Please take care of them," she asked before taking her last breath.

Chapter 21

Faced with Death
Breeze

"Ah, fuck," I yelled as I hopped into my car and sped down the road.

My whole right side was killing me. I felt pain in my ribs and in my right leg. I didn't know where I had been shot and really didn't give a fuck. The greatest thing was I was alive. I hated to leave Tanisha and the kids alone in the crib, but I was sure they would be safe in the panic room. There was no way anyone would even know it existed, and even if they did, there was no way they could get in there.

"Think, Breeze, think," I kept talking to myself as I drove.

I was feeling weak and knew I needed to get help, but I wasn't sure that going to the hospital was the right thing to do. That's when I had to call the only person I trusted, my ma. The only safe place I knew was Grandma's house. I managed to dial my ma from my cell.

"Hey, baby!" My ma said, happy to see my call.

"Ma, I need you. I need you bad, Ma," I said, knowing I needed my mother right then more than I'd ever needed her before.

"Oh my God! What's wrong, Breeze? What's wrong?" Ma started to panic. "Don't tell me the police is after you again?" Ma thought she was reliving her worst nightmare.

The first time I got locked up, I was on the run for months, and when they finally caught up with me I was hiding out at my grandma's crib. The police ran up in the house in the middle of the night with guns drawn. That scared both my ma and grandma half to death.

"No, Ma, I'm hurt. I'm on the way to the crib now," I said, then hung up. I didn't have the energy to say anything more.

Ma was from the streets, so in most emergency situations she stayed calm and did whatever needed to be done. As I looked down at my T-shirt, I noticed it was soaked with blood. I felt like I was starting to lose consciousness but I was determined not to close my eyes. I only had a couple more minutes before arriving at my grandma's crib.

I was thankful when I saw Grandma's house from a distance. I pulled up on the curb, not giving a fuck how I was parked. I dragged myself out of the car and rushed toward the front door.

"Grandma." I barged through the front door, fell to the floor, and literally began crawling across the floor. She was in the living room, watching something on TV

"Oh, Lord," she screamed out.

"Please, Grandma, I need help. No cops or paramedics," I begged before coughing up blood.

"What happened?" Ma asked, grabbing a hot washcloth before dashing onto the floor beside me.

"I'm getting cold," I replied, shaking.

"Boy, I was looking out the side window for you," she explained.

"We can't lose you now. I need you to fight," Grandma insisted.

"I got a plan. Just focus on them grandkids of mine," Ma pleaded.

"Okay," I responded, barely able to move my head. Ma knew that, if nothing else, I would strive to live for the sake of my kids.

Ma and Grandma managed to get me back into the car. As we drove, I heard Ma make a phone call to her longtime girlfriend, Roxanne.

Roxanne was a registered nurse. I heard Ma
tell her I'd been shot and to meet us at the Red
Roof Inn. That's what I loved about Ma, she was
so gangster. She kicked right into motion. She
didn't need any coaching or anything.

It didn't even seem like a whole thirty minutes
had passed before I was laid out across a hotel
room bed with Ma and Roxanne standing over
me. Roxanne shoved some kind of pill cocktail
in my mouth, and gave me a couple of injections.
Then she patched up my wounds. She explained
that the wounds looked worse than they actually
were. I only had a flesh wound on my side and
the bullet went straight through in my leg. She
explained there wasn't any way to be sure if my
leg was broken, but by touching it and by visual
examination, she didn't think it was broken. She
said the only way to know for sure was if we did
an X-ray, and that wasn't gonna happen, so we
just had to take her word for it. Later, Roxanne
explained to Ma how to change my bandages
and when to give me my medication. She'd given
her antibiotics for possible infection, and some
pain medication. Ma spent the next couple of
days with me in the hotel, then she took me back
to Grandma's house. There, they cleaned me

up real good and made sure I was comfortable in bed. I was in and out of consciousness, but I clearly remember Grandma's crying and constant praying for me.

"Good morning, baby," Grandma greeted me while changing the bandages on my wound.

"Did I sleep through most of the night?" I asked abruptly, not able to really remember.

"Boy, you've been asleep for two days straight. The two medicines we've been giving you are strong; but you're healing well," Grandma said.

"Where's Ma at?"

"I'm right here," she spoke before entering into the bedroom. I attempted to sit up but I was too weak.

"It will be a few days before you'll get your strength back," Ma said. "We need to get some food in your system. You haven't eaten, but, we did make sure you had plenty of water and Powerade. Roxanne said to make sure you were well hydrated," Ma added.

"All right," I responded frustrated.

"How about some chicken broth to start off?" Grandma suggested.

"Yeah, whatever," I said, not really caring.

I had other things on my mind. For one, I hated not being able to do what I wanted and when I wanted. This was worse than being locked in a fucking cell. So much shit had gone wrong and everything happened so fast. There were so many people who could have been the ones to cause all this. At this point, everybody was a suspect and I didn't know who to trust. The way I saw it, everybody had motive to set me up. I wouldn't put it past Trixy. I knew she was pissed about how everything had gone down between us. She could have been on some payback shit since I called her out for robbing me. Not only that, she could have done it because of her whole jelousy thing with Tanisha. The way she had gotten all emotional and turned into a psycho bitch when she found out about Tanisha, she probably did it hoping Tanisha would get hurt too.

Then there was Maria. She wanted to be on some baby momma drama shit when she found out about Tanisha. Plus, she was all about the dollars, and you never could put nothing past a greedy bitch. Come to think of it, Maria was at the top of my list as the number-one suspect. She was Biggs's woman. If anybody had the best connect to take drama to, it would have been her.

Plus, Biggs had a beef with me to begin with, so Maria probably didn't even have to try to convince him to go fuck with me. She probably gave him a copy of the keys to the front door of the fucking house. Even Tanisha was suspect at this point. I never really did know what or if she and Biggs had something going on. She would always mention how he would flirt with her every time he came in the bank. Besides, who knows if she was still fucking with that Mexican cat, Jose. She could have planned this up from day one. This nigga Jose was with the Mexican cartel. She could have been his inside worker this whole time and I never would have known.

"Has Tanisha been calling?" I asked my ma.

"Yes." Ma nodded.

"Did you tell her anything?" I wondered just how much Tanisha knew.

"No, I only talked to her once, and quickly had to get off the phone with her to tend to you. All she mentioned was that she and the kids are okay. She was more concerned about you."

"Good," I said, relieved ma hadn't told her anything.

"I was waiting for you to come to so I could ask you what you wanted me to do about the kids. I can call Tanisha and arrange to pick up the kids today if you want. I figure having the children around will cheer you up. I'm sure they miss their daddy, and they probably asking about they momma, too," Ma said

"Yeah, you're right," I said, wondering why Maria hadn't called to check on the children.

"And one more thing," Ma said before taking a pull on her cigarette. "I'm going to say this and then leave it alone, but I think that after all that girl has been through, you owe her some sort of explanation, Breeze. That child is worried sick about you. And not only that, she has been taking good care of your kids these days that you been here with us."

"Ma, not now. I'm gonna call her and explain everything later. But now is not the time," I said, not trying to hear any of all that right now. Not that I didn't agree with what she was saying, but I had a lot of other things on my mind.

"Okay," she blurted out.

"Can you just call Tanisha for me and tell her you gonna come get the children? Put it on speaker phone. I just need to hear her voice, please," I requested. Ma quickly dialed Tanisha's number.

"Tanisha," Ma stated after dialing her number.

"Hello, Ms. Miller, have you heard from Breeze yet?" Tanisha asked, whimpering on the phone. Her voice almost brought tears to my eyes. At that very moment, I knew that girl truly loved me but I still couldn't give in too soon. I needed to sort some things out first.

"No, baby, I'm sorry. Listen, I'm going to pick my grandbabies up today. How are they doing?" Ma questioned.

"They're asleep right now. They're pretty distraught about their mother," Tanisha said.

"What about that wench? Don't tell me she hasn't even called to check on those children."

"Oh, no. Ms. Miller, you don't know, do you?" Tanisha said in a sympathetic tone.

"Know what, Tanisha? Is there something you need to tell me, honey?" Ma asked. From the tone of Tanisha's voice, I already knew bad news was about to follow.

"I'm sorry I have to be the one to tell you this, Ms. Miller. I thought her family would have contacted you all by now. Maria was shot and died at the scene," Tanisha explained.

My heart dropped and I began to gasp for air as I listened to what Tanisha was saying. A knot began to form in my stomach. Maria was a lot things, and I had grown tired of her ass, but she was still the mother of my kids. All kids needed their mother and father. What the fuck was I suppose to do now?

"Oh my God," Ma replied, taken aback. "Listen, baby, I want to thank you for taking care of the kids for me. Let me get your address so I can come get them now. I know you got a lot on your plate," she explained, and then left the room to go write down the information.

"Pray, baby. You've gotta pray. God hears our cries," Grandma tried consoling me.

"I'm good, Grandma. I'm a big boy. I can handle this," I reassured her, then asked for some time alone.

I couldn't believe this was happening. I thought God was on my side. Sure, we had a deal and I'd broken the vow, but I'd always learned God was a forgiving God. Well right then it sure felt like he was getting even with me. He'd taken my kids' mother away from them. Why did they have to pay for all of our shit? None of this was their fault. If God, could do that to them, who knew where my fate lay. Maybe they would end up without a father, too. I laid my head against the pillow and looked toward the right. That's when I noticed a familiar item sitting on the nightstand. There lay the necklace that Moses had made for me in jail. I reached for it and squeezed it tight. I didn't know how it got there, but I was glad it was there. I needed it now more than ever. I pulled the necklace close to my chest and begged God to help me get through this.

"Please, God, you promised you would help me make it. Where are you, Lord?" I prayed aloud.

Chapter 22

Guilt Trip
Trixy

"What you say?" I asked Mannie over the phone before nearly choking on a piece of chicken covered in hot sauce.

"You heard me. We ran up in Breeze's spot. After you gave me that information there was no way I could let that shit ride. We had to show that nigga we were serious."

"Is he dead?" I asked nervously. I expected Mannie and his boys to retaliate, but I never wanted Breeze to end up dead. Maybe at the most rough him up a little bit.

"Nah, but that nigga took a few shots. I heard his wife, Maria, was found dead, though. On the real, niggas don't even know how that shit happened. We thinking Biggs did her in. From what I hear she is the one who told Biggs where we could find the dude in the first place. But the weird thing is that right next to her body, detectives found pictures of her with Breeze. Look like Biggs had a private investigator following her. That bitch was still fucking with that nigga. And anybody who knows Biggs knows he can't stand disloyalty. So if you ask me, Biggs is responsible for her death." Mannie whispered as if he was afraid that if anyone heard him make such an accusation, he would be dead next.

"What about his kids?" The mom in me worried about the safety of his children.

"They all right. They weren't in the crib at the time."

"Oh, thank God," I replied, seeing that Mr. Biggs had no mercy and was probably capable of killing the kids just as he'd done Maria.

"So, now that that nigga Breeze is out of the way, can I come tap that tonight?" Mannie blurted out, always thinking about pussy.

"Nah, I don't have a babysitter. My little one is a light sleeper," I lied, then said good-bye and hung up the phone.

Although I never had babysitter issues because my mom was always willing to keep Junior, the babysitter would always and forever be a classic excuse to get out of doing things I simply didn't want to do. Mannie was the last person I wanted to see. At this point, I regretted even going to him with the news about Breeze. Look what it led to: Breeze getting shot up and Maria dead. All of this was my fault.

I needed to get my head together. My two fried chicken drumsticks didn't look appealing anymore so I threw them in the garbage. Deep down, I was relieved that Breeze was still breathing. I still had feelings for him.

"Ma, who was that on the phone?" Junior asked, coming in the kitchen, rubbing his eyes, just waking up from an afternoon nap.

"A coworker," I said before plopping a kiss on his forehead.

"Oh, I thought you were talking to Breeze. Why don't he come around no more, Ma?"

"Baby, he doesn't live here anymore. I'm sorry you don't get to see him; but at least you have me and Grandma," I said, knowing me or Grandma would never be able to replace a father figure.

"I know, Ma, but I really liked Breeze. He played football with me and took me to the basketball courts. You and Grandma don't ever know how to play PlayStation games. Plus, Breeze got me new Jordans. Aw, Ma, can we go visit him? *Please?*" Junior's begging broke my heart and it nearly made me cry.

It meant a lot to me that Junior asked for Breeze. I knew Junior longed for a father figure, and Breeze was perfect for it. I couldn't deny that Breeze treated Junior like he was his own from day one. Breeze had given my son something that no other man ever had. He was good to my son, and I would always be grateful for that.

Chapter 23

Bloody Murder
Biggs

Home, sweet home, I thought as I drove through the streets of my old neighborhood in Baltimore. I'd come home to lay low for a while to let the event in Virginia blow over. There was nothing worse than regret, and one of my biggest ones was leaving the DMV area. Washington DC, Maryland, and Northern Virginia were my old stomping grounds. I should have stayed there and married my high school sweetheart, Sharon. She was good for me. At the time, though, I didn't realize it. I was too wrapped up in being a young Casanova like so many of the other men in my family. Hell, it was all I knew. The last I heard, Sharon was married, had three kids, and was teaching at a local elementary school. Now compare that to my life: drugs, violence, a cheating woman, and no children of my own. The sad part about this was that I didn't think Breeze or I ever truly had Maria's heart. The only thing that bitch loved was money. To make matters worse, Maria didn't pay those kids of hers any attention until the day I said something to her about it. She would have been happy sending them off to boarding school and traveling the world year-round. Even though I cared deeply for Maria, the truth was that I should have never wifed her up the way I did. I always knew she wasn't the one for me, but for whatever reason, I stayed with her, and days turned into months and months turned into years.

In the end, Maria got what she deserved. She should have known better than to be playing with people's heart. I knew from the time I'd heard that Breeze was home that Maria couldn't be trusted. That's why I wasted no time hiring a private investigator. I knew all about the visits, the gifts, the money, and the cell phone. I even had all her phones tapped, so I heard cell phone conversations and knew all about them having sex. And to think the entire time Maria thought our relationship was going down the drain because I was stressed about the business. The business issues were on my mind a lot, but she had been my main concern. I told her ass from the beginning, just as I'd told every soldier on my team, I don't tolerate disloyalty. Loyalty was the glue that held together any relationship, whether business, friendship, or love. In my book, anyone who was disloyal must pay. Unfortunately, in Maria's case, she had to pay the price of disloyalty with her life.

The truth be told, this was only my second murder. I never was the violent type but some things demanded death, and disloyalty was at the top of my list. Thirty years ago, I had to murder the cat who took my oldest brother's life. Everyone in the area knew my oldest brother loved me more than anything. That was one reason he wanted to keep me out of the drug game. He made sure my tuition was paid in school and that I had everything I needed so that I would never follow in his footsteps. "Esquire," he and his crew would call me, "you monitor what goes on with this here drug game and learn all about it, because you're gonna be the one to get us out of a bind if we ever get caught up," my brother would say as he taught me all there was to know about the game. My brother was very protective of me, so when one of his own men murdered him while sitting at the dinner table, my *Lion King* instincts kicked in. When I got the news, it was almost as though I was in a trance as I walked to the block where I knew I'd find this guy. With no warning, I walked directly up to him, pulled out a gun I'd gotten from my brother's drawer, and fired one shot to his head in broad daylight. I simply walked away, leaving him to bleed to death on the sidewalk.

Chapter 24

Failed Escape
Breeze

It had been two weeks since I'd been shot, and the house was silent on this early Sunday morning. There was no one in the house but me. Grandma had gone to church and had taken the kids with her. Ma had gone to the club the night before and hadn't bothered coming home. The average person would have worried about something like that, but Ma had been doing that shit since I was a child. She would go out, get drunk, and come home with a hell of a hangover late in the afternoon the following day.

A few days prior had been Maria's funeral. I chose not to go, but Ma and Grandma did go and they took the kids. Maria hadn't been buried a whole week before her snooty-ass parents wanted to fight for custody of my kids. I knew that shit was coming. I also knew that unless I made some major changes, I wouldn't stand a chance against them in court. It was time I made some decisions. I was facing losing my children. I had niggas wanting my head. I hadn't seen my P.O. or been to work in two weeks, and I was crippled as a motherfucker. I figured the best thing for me to do at the time was leave. At least I knew this way, Grandma, Ma, and the kids would be out of harm's way. I knew right after the shootout niggas would lay low, but I also knew it wouldn't be long before they were on the hunt for me again.

With that in mind, I struggled to my feet, and threw on a T-shirt and a pair of jeans. Although it had been two weeks, I still was not completely healed. I was moving way too slow. My joints were stiff and everything hurt as I shuffled across the bedroom. I grabbed a duffel bag and put a few things in it. I thought about my family as I packed. I knew Ma would be bitching, Grandma would be disappointed, and the kids would be sad about me leaving without any notice, but I had no other choice. I couldn't leave anything that could possibly be used to track me down. I hoped that down the line they would understand the reason for my actions. I had plans to come back. It was just a matter of when.

With my duffel bag packed, I grabbed my gun, tucked it in my waistband, and headed out the back door. As I took my first step down the stairs I tumbled down. I fell to the ground and was in so much pain I couldn't mange to get up. This was some bullshit. I felt like that old-ass white lady on the commercial yelling, "I've fallen and I can't get up!"

"Godamn!" I yelled, completely frustrated, knowing there was nobody around to help me up. I wondered what the fuck I was gonna do next.

Suddenly, I heard a noise on the side of the house. It sounded like someone was slowly walking toward the backyard. I could hear whoever it was walking closer and closer to me. I managed to sit up straight and prop my back against the house. Then I wrestled my gun from my waist and cocked it, putting one in the head. I gripped my gun tight as I aimed it straight ahead, ready to fire. I could see a shadow the closer the person got. The shadow seemed rather small for an adult body, so I stared closely as a small head peeked around the corner. A smile came across my face as I realized who it was. It was none other than Junior.

"Don't shoot me! It's me, Junior." He stood with his hands in the air, a look of fear and panic all over his face.

"I'm not gonna shoot you, boy," I said as I replaced my gun in my waistband.

Feeling safe now that the gun was away, Junior ran to me and gave me the tightest hug a six-year-old could give. I was glad to see him even though he was hurting me by the second.

"Ah," I screamed out, no longer able to hold in the pain.

"Sorry, Breeze. What happened to you?" Junior asked.

"It's okay. I'm just hurt a little bit. I can't get up," I said.

"Let me help you up," Junior said while trying to lift me with all his little might.

I knew there was no way in hell Junior would be able to help me up, but I didn't want to break his spirits. Besides, that little nigga looked so cute as he grunted while trying to lift me with all his might. I could tell he had such a good heart. I only hoped he never ended up in the streets when he grew up.

"I don't think I'm strong enough," Junior said, disappointed. "Ma!" he yelled out to his mother for help before I could stop him.

The last person I wanted to see was Trixy. I didn't know what the bitch was up to, plus, I was in a weakened state, but it was too late now. I felt a little comfort in knowing I had my gun on me. Worst-case scenario, I would have to put one in that bitch's ass.

"What's going on?" Trixy rushed into the backyard, frantic.

"Breeze is hurt. We gotta help him, Ma. He can't walk," Junior explained. I didn't say a word. I just looked at Trixy with a blank face.

"Let's get you up." Trixy got me to my feet.

"I'm good," I said, now that I was standing.

"No, you're not. You can barely stand up," Trixy insisted while grabbing my hand and bringing me inside her house.

Once inside, she laid me down on the couch and began to clean me up. I hadn't even realized my wounds had started to bleed. *Damn it*, I thought as I lay there. *What the fuck else can go wrong? I can't even make a getaway happen smoothly.* I wondered what I'd done to deserve all this. How could one nigga's luck be so bad?

"You know, Junior made honor roll." Trixy started to make some small talk as she changed my bandages.

"That's good news." I nodded, still not knowing how to take Trixy.

"He adores you, Breeze. He asked about you every day that you weren't here." Trixy's statement really touched my heart.

"I miss that little nigga too," I admitted.

"Well you're all cleaned up now. Let's get you something to eat. You hungry?" she asked while heading to the kitchen.

"A little," I said, still wondering what to make of Trixy's actions.

I didn't understand how at our last encounter she hated me so bad that she busted out all my windows, and now she was nursing me back to health. What bothered me even more was that she didn't ask one question about my gunshot wounds. She didn't ask what happened to me or how I got shot. She didn't even mention if she had heard something on the street. A woman always wanna know every detail about shit and she hadn't asked me nothing . . . nothing at all.

Chapter 25

Inner Struggles
Trixy

Breeze, Junior, and I had been chilling at my house over the past few days. It was just like old times and I was adoring every minute of it. I loved seeing Breeze and Junior playing together again and bonding like father and son. The sight just made my heart melt. There was nothing better than seeing my son happy. That is why, as a mother, I did anything I had to do to give him a decent place to stay, clothes on his back, and food in his mouth. I didn't care if I had to hustle or work a pole to get a dollar, I would do it for the sake of my son. The only place I may have failed him was in providing a father figure, and now it seemed like even that lack had been fulfilled. Spending time with Breeze and Junior as a family had begun to inspire me to do other things.

For a moment, I thought there may be something more out there. Maybe there was a chance of me actually having a family. With those thoughts running through my mind, I quickly decided I wanted to go back to school. When I had graduated from high school, I got my certification as a nurse aid. Taking care of people came naturally to me. So, with that said, I decided that I would go back to school to be a licensed practical nurse.

"Breeze!" I called out to him. I wanted him to be the first person I shared the news with.

"What up?" He walked into the bedroom with a slight limp.

I had been doing my best to nurse Breeze back to health. His wounds had finally started to heal, and he was getting his strength back.

"Guess what?" I said with a big grin across my face.

"You hit the lottery?" Breeze laughed.

"No, silly. I'm going back to school."

"For real? Stop lying." Breeze seemed surprised that such a thing was coming from my mouth.

"For real, Breeze. I want the best for me and Junior. I want to make a good wife for some lucky man one day. I can't just hustle and grind all the time. I need something stable. I'm gonna go back to be an LPN," I explained.

"Damn, Trixy. I never thought I would say this, but I'm fucking proud of you, girl." Breeze gave me a big hug, then headed back into the living room where he had been watching TV before I called out to him.

His approval meant the world to me. Not only did it make me smile, but it made my heart cry. It made me think back to the dirty shit I'd done to Breeze. Every minute of the day I regretted ever having that sit-down with Mannie. I needed to get that guilt off my heart but I didn't know how. I sat in my bedroom, silent, as tears began to fill my eyes.

"What's wrong, Mommy?" Junior had come into my room and noticed my saddened demeanor.

"Mommy's sad." I pulled him near and embraced him.

"Why?" he asked.

"I did something that I shouldn't have done, and I think it hurt someone." I tried my best to explain on a level he could understand.

"You can say sorry," Junior suggested.

"You know what, Junior, that's a perfect idea, but I think this person may not forgive me. Mommy's in a real bad situation."

"You can pray. Grandma says God heals everything." Junior gave another wonderful suggestion. I couldn't believe my six-year-old son had the answer to my despair.

"Excellent idea. We'll pray first. Then I will tell the person sorry and ask him to forgive me."

"Okay. Can I pray with you?"

"Sure," I said, but was afraid I may have needed my son's help with this too.

You see, I had never prayed in my life. I hadn't the slightest idea where to start or what to say.

"We gotta get on our knees," my son directed me.

"Okay," I said, and we both kneeled against the bed. "Dear God," I began to say, not knowing what direction I would go in next. "I never called on you for anything, but I know you exist. If you're out there and you're listening to me, I really need you. I've done some horrible things and it's weighing heavy on my heart. I need you to forgive me and show me the right way, and I need you to give me the strength to ask forgiveness from the person who I have hurt. Please put it in his heart to forgive me." The words flowed from my mouth with ease.

"And bless Grandma, Mommy, and Breeze," Junior added, then we both said, "Amen."

"What y'all doing in here?" Breeze walked in as soon as we'd said Amen.

"We're praying," Junior said, full of excitement.

"You want to join in?" I added.

"Sure." He nodded and carefully got on his knees beside me. Junior wrapped his arms around us. With Breeze's lead, all three of us together prayed to God. It was a beautiful moment, and, for the first time, it was starting to feel as if we could actually become a family.

After praying, I headed to the kitchen to start dinner. I truly believed my nutritious meals and motherly care were nursing Breeze back to his good health. As I prepared dinner, my cell phone rang.

"Hello," I answered.

"You've been sleeping with the enemy," Mannie commented on the other end of the phone.

"Who is it?" Breeze asked, noticing the fright in my face. I shook my head and put my hand over my mouth, letting him know he needed to be quiet. Then I rushed out of the kitchen to my bedroom, where I could be alone.

"Mannie, what you talking about? Listen, I'm not sleeping with anybody. It's about me and my son for now," I insisted.

"If you say so." He busted out laughing and hung up in my ear.

I rushed into the living room. "That was Mannie on the phone. We got to get outta here," I explained to Breeze after making sure I pressed the end button on my cell phone to ensure the call had ended properly.

"You're right, let's go," he agreed while putting on whatever clothes he could find.

We both knew what that phone call meant. We knew it wouldn't be long before Mannie and the goons would be at my house looking for Breeze. I put two weeks' worth of clothes in a suitcase and dropped Junior at my mom's house. Breeze and I decided to go to Newport News and lay low for a while.

Chapter 26

I Mean Business
Biggs

"Mannie, talk to me, I hope you got some good news for me," I stated after answering the phone and placing a few pieces of fried okra in my mouth.

"I know Breeze is with Trixy."

"A few months ago, you were bragging that Breeze was about to make us some money. Then you came to me saying Trixy had given you all this information about Breeze. And now you're telling me these two are together. Mannie, do you really have any idea what the fuck is going on?" I'd heard way too many conflicting stories from Mannie. He was one inch away from being kicked off the fucking team.

"I know it sounds crazy, Biggs. Hell, it sounds crazy to me too. But word on the street is she housing that nigga," Mannie replied.

"Have you been by the house, Mannie?"

"Of course. I went the same night I found out. I've been checking back every day since, hoping I could catch them. But I'm thinking they probably went into hiding a long time ago. Nobody ain't been to the house for days. The house is always dark and the mailbox is full," he explained.

"We got to get that motherfucker quick before the cops come knocking on the door. Use Trixy. A woman is always weak. Go to her brother, mother, sister, cousin, aunt, or uncle to try to track down where she is. Once she finds out we've paid her family a little visit, she will hand Breeze over out of fear. Or, if you're really good, with a little force you should be able to get a family member to talk," I instructed him.

"You know what, I got something better!" Mannie yelled, like he'd come up with a master plan. "Her son goes to the same school as my nephew. I think I'll pay him a little visit. Once we get him, we'll get Trixy, and you'll get Breeze once and for all. This shit needs to be handled and go away." For once, Mannie was talking some shit I was trying to hear.

"Now, you're talking. Get the boy and wait for me. I need to deal with Breeze myself," I declared, and hung up the phone.

***

The next day I headed down to Virginia. It was time my presence be felt again. Breeze had tried to weaken my throne. It was time he knew who was really in charge. With perfect timing, Mannie called my phone as soon as I got in the area.

"Yeah," I answered. "Hope you got, good news."

"We got the boy," Mannie informed me.

"Wonderful, meet me tonight at ten near the docks."

"Okay," Mannie agreed.

I pulled up to the docks about thirty minutes early just to check out the scene. At seven o'clock sharp, Mannie pulled up. To my surprise, Mannie wasn't late. He and the little boy got out of the car and headed to the utility van I was driving. The little boy looked scared shitless. I felt somewhat sorry for him. He reminded me a lot of Jaden.

"Call Trixy," I insisted, pointing to the Trac-Fone I picked up earlier.

"Hello?" she answered.

"We got your son," Mannie revealed.

"Ma," Junior called out.

"Baby, it's going to be okay. Mommy is coming to get you. Mannie, please, don't hurt my son. I'll do whatever you want. Leave him outta this. He's just a child. You got babies of your own," she whimpered on the phone in tears.

"The only way you'll ever see your son again is for a tradeoff. You get us Breeze, and Junior will be back in school by Wednesday," he offered.

"Can I talk to my mom?" Junior asked.

"Of course." I ordered Mannie with a nod.

"Ma," Junior called out.

"Baby, did they hurt you?"

"No. Please tell Breeze to save me. I'm scared, Mommy. I don't want to die, Ma, please," Junior begged.

"That's enough," I commanded, and ordered Mannie to hang up the phone.

Chapter 27

Do or Die
Breeze

"What's up?" I asked Trixy with my hands held up.

"You know exactly who the fuck it was. It was Mannie. Him and Biggs got Junior. I don't know what they doing to my baby. He don't need to be in all of this bullshit. I feel like a fucked-up mother. This is all my fault." She was weeping hysterically in my arms.

"Listen to me, Trixy, please," I urged, holding her in my arms while attempting to calm her down. "Are you listening?" I asked.

"Yes." She nodded.

"We're going to get Junior back. Just follow my lead. Everything is going to work out," I explained while rubbing her back.

I felt like a fucking lowlife. Not only was my children's world fucked up beyond belief; now, I had another innocent child caught up in my motherfucking shit. I knew I couldn't let nothing happen to Junior. I would never forgive myself.

I was ready for war. The way I felt, I'd already lost so much at this point, I was like, "Fuck it. If it's my time to go, so be it." A least I knew I would go down fighting. I figured Ma, Grandma, and my kids were probably better off without me anyway.

I jumped up, grabbed our things, and headed to Trixy's car. She followed me.

"Where are we going?" she questioned once we were in the car. I had decided to drive because she was in no position to.

"One of my spots. I need to handle some business real quick. When I stop by, I need you to stay in the car. I'll be in and out. It shouldn't take long at all. Cool?" I made sure Trixy was okay with being alone for a second before I went in.

I always kept a place that no one knew about. When I say no one, I mean no one, not even Tanisha or my mother. I'd copped that spot under a fictitious name so that nothing could be traced back to me. This is where I kept my drugs, money, scale, and all the incriminating evidence. While in the house, I thought about all the shit caused behind the drug game. When you compare the gain to the losses, that shit ain't even worth it. I shuffled through the house and collected $50,000 from various stashes I had hidden throughout. I placed the money in a duffel bag, then jetted out.

"Call Biggs and tell him that you ready to meet him, but he is to come alone," I instructed Trixy as soon as I got back in the car.

Trixy called back the number that had called her earlier. I could hear Mannie through the phone. "You ready?"

"Yes, I am, but I am meeting with Biggs alone, not you, and no goons," Trixy said just as I'd instructed, her. There was a pause while Mannie discussed Trixy's request with Biggs.

"A'ight," Mannie said. Biggs had agreed to our request. "Meet him at the park nearest to your house at ten o'clock. You know where the spot is," Mannie instructed and hung up the phone.

Although it was only a few hours away, it seemed like days as we waited for ten o'clock to roll around. Back at the hotel, Trixy couldn't stop pacing. I knew not knowing if Junior was safe was killing her inside. It had to be a terrible feeling. I tried my best to console her and assure her things were gonna be all right. But the fucked-up thing is that deep inside, I didn't even know if things were gonna truly be all right. I had a plan but any wrong move could blow the whole thing. I hadn't told Trixy about it yet, because I needed her cooperation, but under the current circumstances she was looking kinda shaky.

"Trixy, I got a plan, but I'm gonna need your help. You think you up to it?" I asked.

"I'll do whatever I have to, to keep the men in my life safe. Breeze, I'm worried about you just as much as I'm worried about my son," Trixy confessed.

"Listen, I stopped by my spot and picked up fifty grand. I'm hoping we can use this as a bargaining tool with Biggs. I'll give myself up as a trade for Junior, but after you get Junior you can offer him the fifty grand for me," I said, knowing the chance of Biggs actually agreeing was slim, but I had to do something.

"Okay," Trixy agreed without hesitation.

"One more thing, here." I handed her a gun. "You never know what he may have up his sleeve. Do you know how to use this?"

"Take off the safety. Put one in the head. Aim and shoot," she said like a pro.

"Perfect," I said, then looked at my watch, noticing the time. "Well, it's about that time. You ready, soldier?"

"Always," Trixy said, then hugged me tight. "I love you, Breeze," she whispered in my ear before letting me go.

I was thrown by her statement. I stepped back and looked her in her face, then parted my lips to ask her if she was serious. Before I could say anything, she placed her index finger across my lips. "Shh . . . don't say anything," she said, then walked away.

I guessed she was right. Nothing needed to be said. I just took in the moment and got my mind back on the war we were about to face. I followed Trixy to the car and hopped in. I grabbed my gun and put it in my waistband. We pulled up to the park a few minutes early. It was dark and no one was in sight. Minutes later, we saw headlights turn on from a distance. We got out of the car and headed toward the lights. When we got near, Biggs hopped out of a black Navigator, with a gun next to Junior's temple.

"Biggs, let Junior go. He's too young for all of this," I pleaded.

"I give the motherfucking orders around here. You got that?" Biggs spat back.

"We got it," Trixy and I said in unison. All she wanted was to have Junior in her arms.

"Both of you need to strip down. I don't want any foolishness," Biggs ordered.

"What!" Trixy stated.

"Bitch, you heard me," he added.

I knew exactly what Biggs was doing. Making us strip was his only way of ensuring that we weren't carrying any weapons. While stripping down, I had no choice but to throw down my gun.

"Apparently, you do follow orders." Biggs smirked, noticing I didn't hesitate to strip down to my boxers.

"Breeze is here as I promised. Could I have my son please?" Trixy pleaded.

"A deal is a deal. Head this way, Breeze," Biggs demanded. I walked toward him as he and Junior started inching their way toward Trixy. When I was near, he released Junior, who ran into Trixy's arms. They hugged each other tight, and, for a moment, it seemed that Trixy had completely forgotten about me.

"I've been waiting for this day." Biggs grabbed me and put his gun to my head.

"Wait!" Trixy yelled. Biggs's words must have brought her back to the situation at hand. "Run to the car," she instructed Junior to be sure he was out of harm's way. Then she continued to speak with Biggs. "I want to make you an offer."

"Yes?" Biggs seemed interested.

"I have money, and I'm willing to give it all to you if you will release Breeze. Not only that, if you let him go I promise you will never see our faces again," Trixy said as she started laying stacks of money on the ground.

"It's about time I recoup some money!" Biggs replied as he walked closer to Trixy in order to retrieve the money from her.

"It's all yours." Trixy put her hand in the bag once again to pull out another stack of hundreds, but this time she came out with a gun.

Bang! One shot to the head and Biggs was down. *Bang!* Trixy didn't hesitate to shoot Biggs in the head twice to make sure that motherfucker was dead. I grabbed the gun from her and we quickly picked up most of the money from the ground. Once we were done, we rushed back to the car. Once inside the car, Trixy hugged Junior so hard his chest started to hurt. I pulled out and sped off, hitting the highway toward the Outer Banks.

Chapter 28

Broken Hearted
Trixy

Once we'd reached the Outer Banks I felt so relieved. We rented a beach house and relaxed, enjoying the ocean. We had been there for an entire week, just laying low. Funny thing was, I didn't miss anything about Norfolk. I had started to wonder if me, Breeze, and Junior could just run away and start over someplace. It seemed like it was all falling into place. It all seemed too easy. I watched as Junior played in the sand while I sipped a cup of hot orange and spice tea, and Breeze drank a Heineken. It was so relaxing, smelling the ocean air and listening to the waves crashing. I felt the timing was perfect; I needed to confess to Breeze and ask for his forgiveness.

"What's on your mind?" Breeze asked, noticing I was deep in thought.

"Breeze, let me start by saying, that I love you so much, and have for a long time."

"Yeah, okay," he said, wondering what was coming next.

"Well, I owe you an apology." I took a deep breath, then continued. "Look, I'm the reason all that beef started on the streets. I told Mannie you had a new connect, and you were working with other people, and you were gonna take the streets over. I was so hurt that day we got into it that I let my emotions get the best of me. I wanted you to hurt like I was hurting, so I figured the only way to hurt you was to hit you in your pockets. I had no idea it would go this far. Will you find it in your heart to forgive me?" I asked.

This time Breeze had done to me what I'd done to him a week before. He placed his index finger across my lips and said, "Shh . . . say no more." Then he gave me a soft kiss on the lips.

That kiss seemed almost magical. It was like no other kiss we'd ever had. It gave me the courage to tell him what I'd needed to tell him for some time. So, without even thinking, I began, "Breeze, I have one more thing to tell you."

"What's that?"

"Junior is—"

"Freeze! Don't move! Get on the ground!" Before I could finish my statement, eight police officers had come out of nowhere and ambushed us.

Breeze and I did as they instructed and got onto the ground.

"Byron Miller, you are under arrest for the murder of Jonathan Stevens, also known as Mr. Biggs," the cop blurted out.

"No, he didn't do it. Let him go! Please!" I begged.

"Yes, I did. I confess to the murder. Please take me away," Breeze stated, and the cops quickly handcuffed him. I was in shock. I felt helpless as I watched them walk Breeze toward one of the cop cars and put him in the back seat. As they drove away, Junior and I held on tight to each other and cried.

Epilogue

Had I made the right choice, taking the rap for Trixy's murder? It was all I could think about that night I was arrested. When I heard those cops say my name, I knew it was all over. I said a quick, silent prayer, and asked God to forgive me for everything I had done. I had messed up so many innocent people along my journey, and I was tired of the life I was living. I felt like taking the rap was my own way of paying for all the pain I'd caused everyone. Now, as I lay up in my bed, all I could think about was if I had made the right descision.

It didn't take long for the news to spread that I was locked up. The letters and visits started pouring in after a couple of days of me being back in here. My first letter was from Tanisha. She'd been on my mind since the incident at the crib, but I never had the courage to hit her up. I didn't know what to say. As I opened her letter, I already knew what to expect. I read the first line. As I expected, she was very concerned about my well–being, but after expressing her worries and concerns came the words, "I'm sorry." What followed was an explanation of why she could no longer be with me. I truly loved Tanisha and I knew she was a good woman, so that's why I knew I had to let her go. After reading the letter I threw it away. I didn't even bother to write her back.

Letters from my mom, grandmother, and kids followed. Realizing I was about to be away from my kids again really fucked me up. My mom never told me she was disappointed in me, but I knew she was. She said in her letters that she didn't have the heart to come and visit me yet, because she didn't think she could handle seeing me locked up again. Grandma, on the other hand, told me straight up she wasn't coming to see me. She said she would never stop loving me and she would pray for me until the day she died, but until I got right with the Lord, she couldn't do much else for me. She told me she was holding the necklace Moses had given me, and when I was ready to where it again, she would send it to me.

Trixy and Junior were the first to visit. I had to admit, I was excited as hell to see them, and they were just as happy to see me. At our visit I got some unexpected news. I found out Junior was my son. I didn't know if that was good news or bad news considering the situation I was currently in.

After our visit I headed back to my cell in a daze. It was time to reevaluate things. As I lay on the bed in my prison cell, I wondered what the hell I'd gotten myself into. It seemed like just the other day I was released from prison, and now I found myself right back in jail again. No, this wasn't the plan I'd had, but it was the life I'd lived. The streets were all I knew. Live by the game die by the game. The game hadn't killed me physically, but sitting in my jail cell I wondered if I could consider myself to still be living.